WATER WARS

BY

Capt. Charley Bartholomay

Copyright 2018
Blue Water Captain
Palm City, Florida
All Rights Reserved

ISBN 978-0-692-19114-9

* * * * * *

The man behind the bar studied the photograph briefly as he ran his leathered hand through his beard. He paused to look away for a second, before giving the snapshot a final glance.

"I tell you again, sir that man has fished around here before, but not for a couple of years now. What his name was…aah…Rob…Robby somebody, my memory not what it used to be, sir. It's been a while since he be back. I pretty much know most of the regular captains and mates that come here to fish, and their boats. There're half a dozen here right now, and they all make it in here sooner or later."

"His name is Radford Kraft; most know him by his nickname 'Crafty.' Some friends back in the States told me this man is here for the next two months for the marlin run. They said if he had any open dates, book him, that he was the only one to fish with, eh."

The bartender had sensed the stranger's act almost from the moment he'd walked into his watering hole; a man on a mission with too many questions, on an island hundreds of miles off the coast of Portugal. You don't come this far to catch a blue marlin on a good boat without making prior plans. The stranger's soft, pudgy white hands betrayed his sport; they had spent too much time gaming indoors, maybe in a Vegas casino during all hours of the night. "So you bring me a photograph, what's your game mister?"

"I just want to charter him for some marlin fishing; you haven't seen him, eh?"

"I do now recall the man's name... Crafty, yes. He was here two years ago on a big Merritt, good fisherman, haven't seen him since," replied the innkeeper as he toweled off the bar.

"I'm over at the Coronado, room 6, how about giving me a ring if he should happen to stroll in, I'll make it worth your while," replied the stranger as he flipped his business card on the bar. He donned his Bean's gentleman fishing hat, and waltzed out the door, perhaps a tad light in the deck shoe.

'I see,' the owner thought to himself, as he walked around and outside the bar into the back room. He opened a louver door housing a converter and a VHF radio, hit the power supply and keyed the mike, "Tortuga… Tortuga.., you on there, Cap'n Mikey?"

"Go ahead."

"Fernando, Mikey. Do me a favor and tell your mate to be sure and drop by this evening around ten, and tell him to come in the back. Got that?"

"All right, Freddie, he'll get the message."

"Mikey, why you starting to call me Freddie?"

"Why…because you speak such good English for an over the hill Portuguese fisherman."

The bartender laughed for only a moment, "Mikey, he finally had the visitor. Don't forget."

"Nope. Seeya Freddie."

The captain hung the mike up on its holder, and stared back out at his bait spread against the mountainous backdrop of the Azores. He'd been hooked by the place the moment he first fished it years ago with his boss from Palm Beach. Even though its spectacular fishing was seasonal, anymore, it provided all he needed. The peace and solitude of the islands in the off months, allowed him to pursue another ambitions tugging within him to write.

Americans came here to fish for Blue Marlin. The season typically lasted seventy five or so days during the months of

August, September and October. The bites were plentiful, and the size and weight of the creatures were exceptional

In late summer, the outer reaches of the Gulf Stream's warm current, push and direct mass quantities of bait into the Azorean Island chain from the west. Huge female marlin gather to feed on juvenile tuna and a sea of squid in continual bulimic frenzy. Feeding, throwing up, and feeding again, the great predators gorge on the enriched chain of life in perpetuity making Roman orgies look like wine tastings.

The somewhat cooler, subtropical waters of the Azores are also visited by larger tuna, Wahoo and other pelagic creatures. But it is the very real promise of getting a shot at a 'grander' blue that brings in the big game fishermen from America and Europe.

In recent years, the invasion of the western fleet was made more practical by a convenient mode of boat transport in the hold of larger vessel. A ship of 700 feet in length had been specifically constructed to carry 1500 linear feet of smaller power vessels that lacked the fuel range to make the transoceanic crossing. It was instantly a highly successful service for owners, who preferred to have their prized fishing boats make the trip on another bottom. The rear door of the 'ferry' was ballasted to enable the Captain to drive right into its open stern, while divers secured and anchored each vessel one by one. A pneumatic grid was then activated to send a series of supports to meet the vessel at its hull. When all riders had been so anchored, the rear door was closed, the ballast pumped out, and the mother ship set off to the east with her little chicks in dry dock.

Mikey's modest 36 footer had made the trip just this way, even though his rig didn't have the speed or comfort of larger custom sport fishing boats more in evidence with each passing year. Privately owned, their crews booked as many dates as possible prior to their arrivals, significantly thinning the charter pool. Still, Mike had time and experience on his side, as no one in the fleet fished more days or caught more blue marlin than he, despite the disparity in the dockside sex appeal of the fleet.

The young couple who had booked the boat yesterday decided to take the boat for another day, having had so much excitement, each having caught their first large marlin. Today their luck had persisted, with a couple of marlin releases estimated to be in the 750-800 pound class. They had found acres of skipjack tuna busting on the surface, running tremendous bait schools into oblivion. The dark silhouettes of the larger marlin were in constant evidence, as they stalked the periphery of the field of death, occasionally breaking into the edge of the tuna, taking the least watchful of the school in an effortless gulp. It was the magnitude of this chain of life that consistently brought all the players to the table in the Azores.

That some years were better than others, that the confluence of currents would once in a while, although rarely, deal the bite to another locale, like Madeira to the southeast, were acceptable statistical probabilities to the marlin chaser. For he is by nature a fanatic, engaged in a hunt with no guarantees, where there are no absolutes. He knows better than anyone when he rises in the morning, he is as much at the mercy of a dynamic ocean's currents as a piece of Sargasso floating in its grip.

Captain Mike leaned over the bridge and motioned for his cockpit ace to join him in the tower. He would miss having such a talent down below for the remaining two weeks of the season, but knew that this would be his mate's final day for this year in the Azores.

"Mikey, you look like you've been working that head too much. Going two for four with a handsome pair for the honeymoon couple not enough for the day, with fresh yellowfin to boot? What do you know that I don't?"

The captain reached into his shorts for his sun stick and began to coat his lips while staring at his mate, not really wanting to say anything at all. "Crafty…it's been a good run, but now it's time for you to book on 'outta here. Freddie just called, there was some dude hunting your ass all over town today, it would appear that you have been located."

"That's it? Maybe an old fishing buddy has come to charter my ass."

"I doubt that, man; they just don't do it that way anymore."

"What else do you know?"

"That's it ol'boy. Freddie says you better stop on by tonight, and use the rear door, please."

The mate stared out over the horizon slowly moving his head from side to side, taking in nothing but the gentle breeze. He had thought to say something, but closed his mouth and hung his head. He went back down the tower ladder.

His captain studied him with great affection as he began to put things away in the cockpit, for the sun was low in the west, and their trolling tack had taken the vessel nearly to the eastern end of the submerged mountain ridge offshore just a few miles south of the island of Faial. From here it wasn't a long run into the town of Horta, and in minutes it would be lines out… in more ways than one. The captain was sure that he saw the shoulders of his mate a little more slumped than before. He began to drift away, when the corner of his eye seized on the quivering lit up tail of the great fish moving in from the right at speed."Right rigger, Blue marlin!" bellowed the captain from up above.

The Mrs., a better angler and always first to the rod, grabbed the standup fifty wide in a blur. Under a relatively light striking drag of about 13 pounds, she began to set herself up in the shoulder harness and gimbal belt, "This one's really taking it, Crafty, I'm going up to the button on him."

"Going to turn right on him, Crafty, four or five hundred and he hasn't slowed since he crashed it. He was as fired up as I ever seen one, must have 220 [volts] running all through him!" Mikey spun his thirty six foot Carolina rig on a dime and buried the throttles with about 2/3 of spool already in the sea to recover. "Have not seen a fish cover ground like this one in a good long while, he still fired up back there!"

As the young bride went to a hearty twenty pounds of drag, she was jerked to the port side of the cockpit due to the chase, whereupon her thighs were braced by the covering board pad and hugged by Crafty as added insurance. "Good Lord," she screamed, "he's burning up the reel!"

At five hundred yards, the fishes' perspective had diminished his size to the onlookers on the boat, but not his speed. His quivering form propelled by his three foot high, lit-up tail, churned through the sea at near interstate speeds. Day-Glo turquoise against cobalt and platinum, the 10 footer only occasionally broke water as if to escape the slip of foam and cavitation.

"You'd better back off that drag some, ma'am, when you get to the bottom or you'll bust him off for sure," Crafty cautioned.

"When I see the aluminum, Crafty!"

Crafty was resigned to watch the end game unfold as he knew it would, knowing the limits of the lighter reel's line capacity. But he had refocused on the creature, and was secretly rooting for its freedom. He was energized, appreciative of the message delivered to him in the twilight of the afternoon. They had been jumped late by a fish which was supremely determined, and particularly gifted in ability and tactical single mindedness. He could gather strength from it all.

With the Tortuga in full chase, throttles in the corner, the great blue had taken them to the knot. As fate would have it the line never reached tensile breaking test, for at the severest of rod bend, the hook merely pulled. Crazy, the mate thought briefly, but not really. "Great fish, Mike, good going. You'd a needed a hairdresser boat to keep up with that creature."

"Wonder how many times he's gotten away with that," the captain thought out loud, "could have been foul hooked maybe."

"Got to love them," Crafty replied smiling at the newlyweds. The mate briefly looked skyward. "Hope I do that well," he spoke softly.

* * * * * *

It was the 'state of the art' centerpiece for the Bureau of Water Management. Six floors of steel-composite and thermal pane office building, built to the highest environmental standards and energy coefficients, sparing no expense in all areas of construction. It was a monument of great beauty, complementing the other buildings that comprised the various state agencies located in the nouveau western environs of Palm Beach County. It was ample testament to the overall health of the robust economy south Florida had been enjoying in recent years.

On the top floor, the Executive Director of the Bureau for Water Management James McCravy was deep in concentration lining up his thirty foot putt on his office green. There was a hundred on his sinking it, double or nothing. The other man in the room remained quiet in time honored respect, not so much for the man but the game.

Big Jim McCravy, as he was professionally known, had risen to power on the traditional, well-traveled pathways familiar to many families of his generation. His grandfather had settled in south Florida in the 1920's, his pioneering spirit eager to set up the battle lines with the gators, snakes and mosquitoes. Through an indomitable spirit, hard work and good boots, Jonathan McCravy amassed a great deal of acreage along the way, parlaying swamp into land that was very suitable acreage for cattle farming and other agricultural purposes.

With more than a little assistance from the Army Corps of Engineers in his journey, by their higher levying of one of the largest freshwater lakes in the world, the Hoover Dike had created a systematic drop of the perimeter water table. This capturing and storing of water greatly altered the landscape of swamps and wetlands into upland grazing pastures and miles of sugar cane fields. There were many negatives, of course, as there always will be when you tamper with nature.

Big Jim's dad was decidedly cracker all the way. And while the entrepreneurial gene seemed to skip across his tenure, the family wealth and holdings did not suffer. It was just that Evan McCravy was content to be a cowboy, and play all day long across the 12000 acres of his ranch. As long as he could hunt and fish, count his money and trap a wild hog with his pit bulls, he was in paradise, and grateful for it. Having no interest in farming, Evan McCravy eventually decided to deed a substantial percentage of his holdings to the south of Lake Okeechobee to the well to do expatriate Cuban families fleeing the Castro regime.

But when the boom came, Big Jim swung the nine pound hammer. His was a world of development and growth; subdivisions and PUDs, going up or going out. He built high up in the sky when allowed, out to the west whenever possible and built cities and towns from nothing, in the middle of nowhere when they let him; whoever 'they' were at the time.

The whole political thing was a natural evolution for Big Jim. He certainly did not need the money, but like many of the rich who were constantly sizing themselves with other rich folk, the better hand is having power and money. Politics equaled shortcuts to Big Jim, a simple act of wealth allocation. He never argued that a rich politician's altruism places some control on the temptations of a career 'dedicated' to public service. The McCravy credo; everyone is greedy. Politicians just have more money, and the necessary, cryptic information to acquire exponentially, that much more.

Having settled himself free and clear of all yips, Big Jim initiated the tender back sweep of his cherished putter, only to be startled by a louder than necessary page from his secretary. His blood pressure skied immediately as his freckled, precancerous Scottish skin turned beet red. The irritated executive reached over and keyed the office intercom, "yessss, Caroline."

"Chuck Del Gato on line 2, sir."

Taking his seat to allow his knees respite from holding up some 350 pounds, Big Jim hit the speaker phone as he briefly glanced over at his ten thirty appointment, "Charley, do you have me well placed for the weekend?"

"Four collegiate… all handpicked homecomings, and four pro parleys. Let me know your pro layoffs by Saturday night at eleven. I'll receipt your cards by Fed X."

"Del Gato, you're the man."

"Only for the moment, you better tidy up by the end of the week is what I've heard."

"That's ridiculous. This is the best endowed slush fund in the entire country," snapped McCravy in a moment of ignorance, "this is purely for entertainment."

"I'm not as worried as some people," replied the speaker, "but I would get thee straightened out with the 'accountants' sooner than later."

"Yes, dear….I'll let you know by Saturday. Bye."

Big Jim ran his fat fingers through his thinning hair before smiling quietly at the man across the desk, "My bookie."

"What exactly is your job description around here, McCravy, the weight on your shoulders seems almost too much to bear," the man observed with a time proven grin.

"Adam, my mission is simple. Buy and control as much raw land as possible, and make sure any other land owner can't fart without our permission. You know, creatively get yourself in the way of everything that happens in 'controlled quality growth'. What a job, what a bureau, what a country!" They shared a laugh. "So…this somehow brings us to the reason for your visit here today. According to our conversation last week you felt you had all these tech companies in your hip pocket, and that it is your plan to build your little Silicon Valley right here in Dixie, or a few miles from here, that it?"

"In the grand scheme of things, that would be close to correct, Jim. All that one ever reads regarding development in Florida is how much they want to lure the soft industry of the tech sector into the state, you know, the environment, it's the environment."

"Mr. Wendt, that's what we have the Army Corps for, Dammit!" Big Jim broke into sustained laughter, his huge belly heaving up and down. His laughing soon evolved into a wet wheeze, however, and Adam Wendt briefly considered he might lose his precious connection at any moment.

McCravy opened a desk drawer and retrieved a bottle of Dickel sour mash, pouring a good shot into his empty coffee mug. In the top drawer he pulled out a vial of pills, emptying a little white one in his palm before downing it with the bourbon. "Preventative maintenance, Adam…the good old Corps, guardians of the environment, earth movers and shakers, scapegoats and all round horror show."

"Hmmm. Jim… I understand there is already a contract on those 8000 acres of Bud Aiken's ranch a little northwest of here. I spoke with the broker, he assured me they were going to go hard at the end of the month, a land bank by a syndicate from Chicago and Atlanta; they want it for hunting, each partner getting a share of the overall tract."

"Yes, I know all about it, Adam, we own some subsurface rights under a bunch of it. Nice piece, lots of trees, lots of game, a few springs, and…a few wetlands. The broker is an old timer that couldn't close a door. I've dealt with him before, had to undercut him a few times myself." Big Jim sought to redirect, presenting himself in a more mentoring posture, but he could not conceal his inner joy, "Adam, contracts come and go, but they're not worth a single ply of toilet paper if the right people don't say 'go ahead'."

"I really want that property, Jim, in no uncertain terms. The subsurface rights…I hope that isn't going to interfere with our plans. Oil, phosphate…what?"

"Rock."

"I see, but I fail to see the humor in-"

"Coquina rock, boy, a few hundred million dollars of it lying underneath all that dirt."

"I'm afraid I'm a bit confused, Mr. McCravy."

"Good thing you don't build roads, walkways and high end residential patios for a living, Adam. Coquina rock is money in an engineer's hands, hard firm ballast but pliable and its drainage quality surpasses all others. You stick to preaching to the yuppies and leave the rest to me."

"As I said, there is a contract on it."

"It'll never fly, Adam, unless of course, we decide that it's time to give it the gas. You have any idea how damn easy it is to gather environmental support for land preservation around here? It's easier than finding a hooker in Havana for crying out loud. Speaking of which, I might very well have to consult with the sugar folks." Big Jim drifts off for a moment of reflection.

"We'll do well, Mr. McCravy, very well indeed."

"I don't do the deed otherwise, sir," a suddenly serious Big Jim intoned. "Adam, don't be talking to anyone else about what you heard here this morning, nobody. Give me a call in a month; I have a lot of shit to do. Bye."

"I'll be in touch, Big Jim," replied Adam as he rose to look the executive in the eye, "I'll keep you out, you keep me out."

Big Jim remained seated, and he didn't even bother to look up as he scanned his morning news in silence.

* * * * * *

The first point of contact was the pure whistle of a predawn cardinal; the clear ascending tone gently coaxed the man out his unconsciousness. The captain let the aroma of the dew heavy swamp fill his soul as he began a long, sustained stretch. The strong scent of live oaks, night blooming jasmine and scrub pine permeated his cabin. He shifted to his left side to crack an eyelid to take in the early pink heavens to the east.

Captain Louis peeled off the covers, leaving his blond bed partner still in her slumber as he slowly rose to his feet. Naked, he walked out the cabin door for a better look at the emerging day, drinking in the sensual through every pore. The pink cirrus clouds had now transformed to a brilliant gold selectively illuminating the broad savanna that was awakening before him. This was his chosen sanctuary, his refuge. He often referred to it as 'the land that time forgot.' It was his youth, his love, a lifelong romance with the creation, and as he often dreamt, his place to die. It was appropriately named, "Lake Eden."

The air was thick enough to see, as it layered a few yards over the swamp. He gazed out at the mirror of water, its glass surface occasionally penetrated from early fish activity below. A grunt from a gator echoed across the pond, answered by a deeper grunt surprisingly near his position on the eastern shore.

A couple of blue herons had perched themselves on advantageous trees, motionless in their study of baitfish schools imperceptibly dimpling the lake waters below. As the light rays finally angled down to the water, the first splashes and sounds of predatory bass strikes blew revelry to the remaining citizens that breakfast was underway.

Louis walked back up the path to the cabin to grab his bait caster, with hopes of grabbing his bride as well, to see if they might happen upon a couple of fish this fine morning. She was stirring as he opened the screen door, her soft sleepy smile widening as she peeled off the sheet, "Morning, Captain." The bass could wait a few more minutes.

"Right under that clump of pickerel grass, Cami, there's a good one living there. I've been watching her for a few days now; she's getting all she needs hunkered down right there. She doesn't need to even get off the couch with all the bait coming and going from the deep water to the flat behind her. Get that little twitch bait as close as you can, sweetheart, she might jump you, although I think she might want a bigger morsel."

"Don't get yourself all worked up so early in the morning, Louie, it's bad for your heart."

"Little late for that, ain't it?"

"You just watch." She underhanded the soft plastic bait within an inch of the stump of bladed green stems, letting it rest for a second or two before giving it a slight gentle twitch. Without breaking the water's surface, upwelling currents by the large bass' movement below swirled the water all around the lure leaving it unmolested in time. She casted again and again but nothing could trigger the bite. After about twenty such presentations, she laid the rod down in the jon boat, put her hands behind her head, leaned back and silently smiled at Louis. "Well?"

Louis picked up the rod and heaved a long cast onto the lily pads covering the shallower flat beyond. He slowly worked it across the mat of bonnets until he found a clear opening, upon which he let the lure be still. Seconds later, a slight twitch was all it took to get the two pound bass to crash the bait as it cleared the water. Louis raised up on his rod tip, rising to his feet in one motion as he quickly lifted the juvenile fish again into the air, spanking it across the dense pads to the edge of the flat and that stump of pickerel grass. And there and only there was that fish allowed back in the water.

Funny thing, though. The fish suddenly liked it more out of the water, and went immediately on his tail. Underneath, Grandma Largemouth opened her mouth and flushed the toilet, taking the two pound bass on his descent along with half the clump of pickerel weed and a few gallons of water.

"Good Lord, Cap, somebody drop a bowling ball over there!"

"I don't know if I got enough exposed hook, Cami, but here goes." Louis dropped his rod tip while quickly cranking up all the slack, once again rearing back somewhat violently to maybe grab hold of this old girl if only for a few seconds. And now, it's Grandma up on her tail, opening those trademark lips wide enough to accommodate a volley ball. She is off when she hits the water as fourteen pounds of Florida Black Bass straight lines it into the maze of lily pads, pushing water all the way. The reel is screaming and five pounds of drag cannot stop her. She has managed to vector all over the wide flat, taking large clumps of bonnets, uprooting them as she goes. Louis looks down at his reel and he is nearly out of line, but she has for the moment, stopped taking it. "Whatcha' got on here, Cami, 14 pound?"

"Not heavy enough, huh?"

"Well, she might still be there, but I could never give her the heat to contain her. Let's go hunt her down." Which they did, yard by yard, clearing uprooted pads as they went, unwrapping the monofilament tangle in a variety of directions. In a half hour, they got to the end of the line, where the hook had found a permanent home in a submerged cypress stump a foot off the bottom in the three feet of water covering the flat.

"Fish one, Cuban Louie nada."

"That's cool, getting the bite was a blessing all its own."

"I thought the point of all this art was to catch 'em, Louie."

"The point of all this is to be some small part of it."

"I hear you…I'm only taking advantage of what little opening you give me, silver fox."

"Old Dog."

"Naah! I've already taught you one new trick today."

"That you have, Cami that you most certainly have. Hungry?"

"Yes I am."

And so the captain let his soon to be bride row the two of them the 200 yards back to shore. Louis hopped out and dragged the old aluminum boat far enough up on the sand where a quick hard rain would not cause the lake to reclaim it.

The two grabbed their gear and headed up the path to their temporary home, a lakefront guest cabin the owner of the property had constructed for his oldest son and soon to be daughter in law prior to their wedding day. They had never taken occupancy, however, as the young man had never returned from his second tour of duty in Viet Nam.

Bill McDade Jr. was one magnificent bastard. He most certainly was. Facing completely insurmountable odds, he was struck down along with the majority of the 'magnificent bastards,' the most celebrated marine unit in the Viet Nam war. Only a hundred had held a position against thousands of Viet Cong, for days and days. Leading his platoon out along a river against the 'wishes' of his diffident young CO, he spared the lives of many of his brothers, though he did not come out with the chosen few.

His father, William McDade had dedicated this beautiful little nest on the lake and the few citrus trees around it, to his son's memory. Although the cabin is rife with memorabilia, photographs and other treasures that grandfather, father and son had shared, he had never spent the first night in it. After senior Jack McDade's passing, the surviving brothers Bill and Beach saw to it that the cabin would remain pristine in its condition as a memorial and retreat for the family. There was nothing like it anywhere in all the Savannas.

Louis took a quick detour to pick a few of Indian River's famous citrus, sweet Valencia oranges and a couple of ruby red grapefruit. They were the finest oranges in the world, better than their reputation growing not fifty feet from his temporary residence. And therein was the rub, that word 'temporary.' For Louis knew all too well that his time within the sanctuary was indeed, borrowed. He would not expose his old friend to the very real danger that was threatening to overtake him and Cami; a final stroke meant to dispose of all the threads that could lead to the truth behind the murder of his former boss, Frank Whitman. He was deeply thankful for this provision and grateful to Bill McDade for the generous gift of this cabin. With his new gal, he knew that this was the very best this life had to offer. He would savor each day, as he studied his options with regard to extricating himself from the legal and threatening situation his boss's murder at sea had created.

Frank Whitman had been his friend. With honor and loyalty, he had given his life so all others on the boat could survive an attempted piracy at sea. What would have been a victory celebration at Marina Hemingway in Santa Fe west of

Havana, wound up being a murder and a foiled kidnapping at sea. Betrayed by his own aide, Scott Byrd, the trap had been set for an inside-out piracy off the shores of Cuba. Against tremendous odds, Louis, his mate, Crafty and Frank had undermined the attack by regaining control of the boat in spite of being held at gunpoint with assault weapons and proprietary communication devices. It was Frank, who already wounded and bleeding heavily, that made the crucial decision to rush the gunman. The sudden lunge at Scott Byrd gave Crafty the time to produce a concealed lip gaff and eventually dispatch the onboard attacker, hurling his lifeless body overboard. Surely, Frank knew he was going to take a good portion of that clip. He was killed instantly.

The remaining three, charged by the oncoming attack vessel, had managed to regain control of their boat. Knowing that their radioed position and GPS coordinates had been used to create a critical visual reference point for a cut in the reef, Capt. Louis allowed the boat to slip off that critical point using the set and drift of a swift 'down' current. Inexperience and a couple of flaws in their attack plan completed the task of leading their pursuers hard aground up on the reef.

Hidden from view, operating the boat by an autopilot remote control, the three provided no targets and passed by the stricken vessel at running speed, but not before taking a good deal of fire. They limped their way back to Florida across the straits, and finally back to Marathon. By the grace of God, they had survived the piracy, although most of the evil scenario had achieved its goals. A computer icon had been eliminated, his future resources decimated, chaos had prevailed throughout the industry, and the stolen technology had greatly appreciated in value.

Louis had lost a good friend, but gained a love. Crafty had split for international fishing destinations, blindly playing a game of cat and mouse with the shadows, wondering when someone really would emerge from the dark, to slit his throat, or take a sniper's stance from an unseen location. The mate understood that the contractor of this high reaching gambit would not rest until the surviving three were dead. That was the only closure that a diabolical predator like Adam Wendt would accept.

Louis knew their whereabouts were unknown for the moment, but he and Cami were prepared to leave at a moment's notice, having already devised an escape plan through the swamp. The captain knew Wendt had amassed great power and connections, amplified even more by recent successes. His vast network would almost certainly locate them sooner than later.

Adam Wendt had instilled a healthy fear in the mind of the old captain. For as much beauty and good the world and creation gave witness to, he was not blind to the true amount of evil ever present within it. There were many beasts prowling around, seeking only the souls of men.

The pair loaded up with some fruit, finally making their way back to the cabin via the overgrown path. As they approached the small landing at the front door, Louis saw that someone had left a note and stuck it in the screen door. "Hope all is well and you two are enjoying the place-will stop by later this afternoon. Bill."

"He is such a quiet guy, Louie, pretty decent of him to let you crash here for a while."

"Us."

She smiled, "Right. Does he know?"

"Probably… bits and pieces. I need to sit down and let him in on everything, got to do that; maybe this afternoon if I get the chance.

                              * * * * * *

Freddie's joint was approaching peak activity as it was just around ten that night when Crafty made his way through the back door of the bar. Folks on the island usually ate dinner around this hour as was the long held custom. It was more of a happy hour time than a late dinner hour, with most of the fishing crews hoisting a few drinks along with many of the locals. Fernando's joint was the premier watering hole in Horta, and this evening it was filled.

Crafty rapped on the door leading out to the bar from the back room. Freddie checked his watch, laid the bar rag down, and told his third of as many wives to mind the store for a while. She winked in acknowledgement as he passed her to go into the back room.

He greeted his friend with a smile as he entered and motioned him over to the door, cracking it ever so slightly to provide Crafty with a narrow view of the man he had first met that afternoon.

"That's him in the Eddie Bean hat?"

"That's him, amigo."

"You got to be kidding, this is the thug that asshole sent to do me."

"My friend, you of all people should know that in matters such these, all is not what is appearing to be."

"A very good locution, Freddie. I might have expressed it a bit differently, but your point is well taken." 'He was right,' Crafty thought to himself. In fact, Wendt's inside muscle, the diffident Scott Byrd, had presented himself in much the same manner. 'He's dead' thought Crafty with a smirk, don't get sloppy and don't form any opinions. "You know, Freddie, you don't have to be big and strong to squeeze a trigger."

"Crafty, how it is said, God created all men, but Sam Colt made them equal."

"Getting better, Fred, getting better. Freddie, I think I'd like to buy that man a drink, but I'm not sure, know what I mean?"

"Yes, Crafty, you let me know, I make him local special."

"Well, introduce us for crying out loud."

"Hold on, I tell him I not see you here!"

"No, I just flew in to meet my boss from Palm Beach to fish the last few days, just a coincidence. It won't matter, Freddie."

"I don't want trouble with this man, Crafty."

"It's me he wants, amigo, he wants nothing to do with you or your country. Believe me."

"It is so."

The pair walked back into the dimly lit bar over to the table where the inquiring stranger was nursing a double 12 year old scotch. The man from Ocean City rose to his feet.

"Mister…ah?"

"Charles Brewster...from Ocean City…New Jersey that is."

"Senor Brewster, to much my surprise, may I now present Senor Crafty, who this very day flew in from Florida to meet his jefe from Palm Beach for fishing, yes?"

"Crafty, how are you doing, call me Chet like everybody," replied the man with a broad grin, "been dying to meet you, I want to go catch me a grander blue if you got any openings this week. My fishing buddy in Cape May said you were the only guy to go with!"

"And he would be?"

"Ricky Salazar. You must know Ricky he's all over the place. Down in Venezuela right now chasing the white marlin around."

"Sure, I know Ricky Ricardo, that pecker head's chasing a whole lot more than whitey around down there." They shared a laugh as Crafty took the man's extended hand and started pumping it hard and vigorously. Brewster's grip felt like cold, damp smooth rubber. "I'll have to check my book and confirm with the boss man, but I think we can have you out on the rip sometime this week. Where are you staying?"

"The Coronado…here, take one of my cards…room 14. "

"Today's couple had some decent action; nice scenery too, might split the boat with you tomorrow. They've been fishing a couple of days already, might want to go one more."

"Appreciate that, really do, but…when the big boy shows up, I want the shot. Nah, don't like crowded cockpits, I'll just book the charter alone, if that's alright, Crafty."

"Not a problem, Chet, I understand exactly where you are coming from. How many marlin have you caught, sir?"

"Not nearly enough, maybe ten or so blue ones and a bunch of whites, mostly in the canyons offshore Jersey."

"Where have you had most of your bites, which canyon?"

"Crafty, I can never remember one from the other, sorry. The Poorman's maybe, getting old. I did catch three in one day off St. Thomas. Don't have to run quite as far."

"How far?"

"In St. Thomas…around the corner from Red Hook Marina a few miles or so."

"Chet, let me go check my calendar, and call the boss and see when his guests arrive. We'll sure try to get you out there if you can give me a few minutes. Fernando, can I use your phone?"

"In the back, Crafty, I show you."

They exited into the back closing the door behind them.

"That dweezil has never been fishing a day in his life, Freddie. If he knows Ricky, it's for all the wrong reasons. I had dinner with Ricky one night in his Brigantine castle on the Jersey Shore, can't see these two as fishing buddies." Crafty lifted the phone, and immediately began the tedious process of dialing Jackie Dial, who, as of yesterday, was still the Captain of the Concrete Reef, Mr. Richard Salazar's 56 foot custom sportfish. After many minutes, a scratchy but acceptable connection had been established.

"Yeah?"

"JD, Crafty, what's 'shakin'?"

"Crafty where the hell you been?"

"Over here in the Azores, doing a little trolling."

"Catching?"

"Forty four, two maybe looking at a grand; we're not stroking nothing anyway."

"Hot, man!"

"Look, JD, I don't have a lot of time. Where's your boss right now, down in Venezuela or something?"

"Not this year, he's been up in British Colombia fly fishing with his new bride."

"What another one?"

"You would have thought he'd learned his lesson by now, the last one almost got the boat."

"Yeah…British Colombia, huh. Thanks JD, I have got to fly. I'll catch up with you at the Buc when I get back to Palm Beach."

"Do that ol'boy and don't forget to duck. Seeya."

Crafty hung the phone back up on the wall in a moment of reflection before turning to the bartender, "Here's twenty for the call, I'd like to buy Mr. Brewster that toddy, Freddie. Load it up."

"Yes, Crafty, and you are now gone?'

"Yes, old friend. I won't tell you where either, it's best that way. When I leave here tonight, I'm gone until next time. Hasta luego, Freddie." The two men embraced briefly before the mate went back out and sat down.

"Tell you what, Chet, how bout day after tomorrow?"

"Hey, now you're talking. It's official."

"Cool. Let me buy you another drink. Scotch is it?"

"Thanks, Crafty, a double Johnny Black with a splash."

"Freddie, another double with a splash of water for my angler!"

"Double Johnny Black with a splash," yelled Fernando. The barkeep grabbed a tall glass and poured in a generous measure of the good stuff. He then grabbed a small bag of ice from the recesses of the freezer, and a small bottle of water from another corner of the bar underneath the bar top; a special draw of water from the volcanic spring in his backyard. Lovely, and sweet tasting right out of the ground with one particular distinction; it was so laden with minerals it had a telling visceral reaction in the human gastrointestinal system. It would give a barium enema a run for its money. And the ice-cubes, made from the same water. Throw in a parasite or two and you've got a one-two punch guaranteed to krazy glue Chet Brewster, or whoever he was, to the toilet for an undetermined amount of hours, or until the antibiotics kick in. By then Radford Kraft would be long gone.

"For the gentleman, Johnny Walker, for the pirate, Anejo and Coke."

"To the grander," toasted Crafty.

"To the grander," echoed Brewster. The chubby man took a surprisingly long pull, even chewing a couple of cubes along the way. "I very much appreciate your working me in, Crafty"

'Out' the mate thought. "Tell me, Chet, what's the longest you've ever been on a fish?"

"Couple of hours."

Well you ain't getting out of this chair for a lot longer than that Crafty thought to himself. "The name of the boat is the "Dominatrix, it's a 58 American. Unless you brought your own rigs, we got all the tackle you'll need. Another round, Freddie."

"What time do we untie the lines," asked Brewster shifting in his seat a little, "I did bring a couple of sticks and some other shit that I want to bring on board."

"Eight. We'll have the engines running when you get there, just bring your lunch and gear."

"I might bring a gal friend, I'm not sure," said the man now really shifting around uncomfortably in his seat. And then, that look of doubt that began to spread over his face, "Thank you for everything, Crafty," Brewster droned after downing the rest of his now 3000 year old scotch, "I think I'll just let myself out…is there another door other than the one in front?"

"Roger. Down the hall right there," Crafty pointed.

"Thanks again."

"The pleasure was mine, Chet." Crafty could barely hold it together as the man backed himself right out of the room. Crafty wasn't too partial to the man's dinner selections, though.

* * * * * *

Hatteras Village had certainly seen its share of growth in recent years. The beach development that had invaded Nags Head to the north, had been working its way south towards Buxton and Cape Hatteras Light a little further each year. Still, from Hatteras Village on down to Ocracoke, there remained a shred of isolation. For in its creation, the outer banks of North Carolina were nothing more than a series of sandbars thirty miles out to sea. From that stretch of beach, the Gulf Stream's northerly warm current could be accessed as it constantly pushed north, a mere 23 miles due south of the sea buoy at Hatteras Inlet. A fisherman seeking its blue water treasures would have to travel hundreds of miles south, all the way to Florida's treasure coast to find the Gulf Stream in such close proximity.

To further understand Cape Hatteras as a unique fishing destination, one need only look at the entire southeastern seaboard of the United States and the structure of the continental shelf offshore. From the Gulf Stream's origins in the Caribbean sea and the Yucatan Channel through the Florida Straits around to Stuart and finally northward towards the outer banks, the northerly warm current directs the many migrating pelagic creatures to cooler summer waters.

On the east side of the Bahamas, the features of the continental shelf also play a significant role in these migrations. At Hopetown on Elbow Cay in the out island Abacos, structure abounds. There is a prominent point offshore the island, leading to a series of canyons and ridges further to the east. But of real interest is the ocean slope itself, the ocean floor as it were of the south

Atlantic. From about 24 miles east of south Man 'O War Cay, all the way to the 30 fathom 'rock pile' due south of Hatteras Inlet, an ocean slope bottom break that could almost be drawn with a ruler, save the area around the Blake Spur. Most migrating game fish eventually pass to the east of Diamond Shoals offshore Cape Hatteras, guided by the Gulf Stream current.

Once around the Cape, the migrating fish would soon be distributed among the many offshore canyons that define the continental shelf and its drop off in the offshore waters of the northeastern United States. The Norfolk, Washington, Poorman's, Baltimore, Wilmington and Hudson are all names familiar to the experienced 'canyon runner.' The current eddies these undersea structures create; interact with the colder, nutrient rich inshore waters to lure great schools in the bait chain. The end result of course, brings in the predators.

As summer moves into fall, this pattern will shift eastward to outposts such as Bermuda, the Azores and Madeira. Creation and creatures in perpetual motion, being directed to feed and reproduce in the most ideal situations, locales and water temperatures. The experienced fisherman lives intimately with the knowledge of this precision. For it is said, 'the ocean is a place with its life underground.' Even with the better eyes that technology offers the fisherman, it is still by faith that the fisherman sets his lines. He doesn't get to scope the game that often.

The old timers always have more stories of bigger catches, nothing new under the sun there. But Pamlico Sound still provided a bounty for the various pound netters, and the pots still held a good deal of crab. Offshore, something is always going on. Even in winter, the inshore wrecks from Hatteras to Morehead City provide a good opportunity to get a shot at a giant Bluefin tuna. Hatteras Village was still a fishing town inhabited primarily by fishermen, of varying sorts.

The Cedar Island ferry ride outside of Morehead City marked the beginning of the homeward trek for Crafty. Once he hit the sound, the sensual took over, the sights, the smells and the 'feel' of the air, the bluebird skies streaked with high cirrus clouds, the sweet smell of Pamlico Sound. He knew he would find his home not as he left it ten years ago. His parents were both gone, his brother had moved on to Virginia Beach and had never returned. He had only a few friends to see, and a couple of places to go. He had no idea how long he would be here. He did know that he had to see it one more time in the event things took a turn for the worse.

He made his connection for the short ride into Hatteras at Ocracoke Island, before traversing Hatteras Inlet and Bird Island, and finally into the ferry dock at the southwest end of the island. He took his time driving into town; there weren't exactly a lot of miles to be covered. He passed by Teach's Lair and was awestruck with the development of numerous condos and the greater number of boats in the basin which had become much larger than he remembered.

When he came upon Hatteras Harbor he pulled over to the right for he really didn't want to go searching through the marina just yet. He was amazed to see so many boats and condos where there once was a simple fish house.

Crafty got out of the car to take in a long gaze at his youth. The condos dissolved, the 60 and 70 footers all turned into 40 ft. single screw Carolina rigs, and the whole western side of the marina once again transformed into pasture giving an unobstructed view of Pamlico Sound. He saw the lone double wide trailer that was Hatteras' Harbor's first dock office. He opened the door, and found his old friend Jim Burns behind a simple desk, doing his best to get everyone out on the charter boats; and the sign above the man, it read, "Welcome to Cape Hatteras, where if the whole world ended tomorrow, it would take three days to find out." 'So simple, so beautiful, and now so complicated, so techy, so smothering', Crafty thought to himself. He longed for those earlier days.

A brief drive through the village had him at the entrance to the Marlin Club, a somewhat hidden road on one side of the main grocery in town.

The dock had but few vessels tied up, being the time of year and all, but one boat immediately caught Crafty's eye. As he walked behind her and stood at her transom, the logbook in his head began to retrieve some of the memories of good days on the rip with her Captain and owner. The 'Brothers Pride,' she was an Omie Tillot, with beautiful lines, a boat that could run head seas with the best of them. The Greek had requested to keep the name the original owners had given her and was pleased they had no problem with that.

"Crafty, you Palm Beach cur, what brings you back to this sandbar!" The man leapt up on the covering boards, over to the dock, picked the mate up and gave him a huge squeeze. "How 'ya doing bro, what are you doing here? I heard some shit about you and Louie that seemed like just that….you on the run?"

"You could say that, Emory. Some of that stuff you heard was probably true, although we were both cleared of any criminal acts. It's just that contractor wasn't able to finish the job."

"What job, man?"

"Louie and I were incidental catch to a far more ambitious plan. We got in their hair a little bit, screwed up their tactics and best laid plans, and left them with a couple of messy details to clean up. So, Emory, I've been keeping a low profile as of late. But what about you, the Greek still own this rig?"

"Due in tonight, wants to make the trip down to Palm Beach with me."

"Traveling alone?"

"I'm sure the Gloves will be with him."

The Greek…really an Italian who thought he could elevate himself a notch, by taking his origins out of town. 'Gloves' was his body guard of 12 years, about 235 pounds of ranking heavyweight, who never tired of personal training. His hands were the size of a marine battery, he need only get you once, and you were down. "Want to make the trip, Crafty?"

"Got this rental car…tell you what, I'll meet up with you down there. Have you got anything going for the winter?"

"The 'Buc' is all, kind of thin this year. You lined up with anything? Love to have you, and I know I speak for the boss."

"Pencil me in Emory. I'll do it. I'll give you a call when I get back to Florida, but I'm in, definitely."

"Cool ol'boy. I'm holding you to it. Hey, man, boss' plane supposed to be in at Billy Mitchell in thirty minutes, got to meet him with the jeep." Emory again put his hands on the mate's shoulders before shaking his hand a final time. "This was a good case of timing, Crafty. Your luck is just starting to change. Take care of yourself will you."

"I will Capt. Dillon. Looking forward to fishing with you again. Give my best to the Greek."

Crafty meandered down the rest of the dock, as he watched his friend pull away out of the parking lot. His mind was really working overtime now, and he could feel the beginning of a plan coming to the surface. "I believe you're right Capt. Emory. This was a good stroke."

The mate made his turn back down the dock, wondering who he could go harass at the Hatteras Marlin Club. 'I wonder if Homer is still running this place.'

* * * * * *

As soon as Adam Wendt closed the door to his office Big Jim McCravy put down his newspaper and picked up the telephone to give his field manager a call. "Sammy boy, where are you?"

"Up here at the northwest end of the Loxahatchee doing some soil analysis, the drainage here seems to outfall toward the north for some reason. What do you need?"

"How long ago did we finish up with the comments regarding the Aikens ranch?"

"I don't know…hell, Jim, that was months ago, now what?"

"I need you to go up there and reexamine the area, especially after all this rain, it has been a pretty heavy storm season you know, I'm sure there might be some issues we may have overlooked."

"Issues, I thought we were done with that guy."

"Listen up, Sam, that Contract is set to go hard in a matter of days, and close within the next thirty. At the very least, we have got to play for a little time if, we want to redirect the piece."

"I don't know Jim; we're way far down, no… beyond the approval process. I don't know what you got up your sleeve, but it smells like trouble."

"What I'm telling you, Sammy, is for you to get your ass up there and find some issues. There are always issues with retention, runoff and drainage!"

"Easy, Big Jim, easy. Can you get me permission?"

"Absolutely not."

"Are you ever going to leave me alone, McCravy?"

"You want to go back on your old salary?"

"You're something you old bastard! Give me few days to go over my field reports. Are you sure I can't just call McDade for access to the property, I mean he's a pretty level on the level guy."

"I don't want him to know understood? Get moving now!"

"Okay, Jim, but this is the last time, you understand me?"

"Bye, Sammy, you know that I do."

The November morning had already taken a turn towards the heat from a light southwesterly breeze, and Beach McDade had sweat pouring down face. Having spent the first part of his life in south Florida without the advent of AC, he had just grown accustomed to living without it whenever necessary. His rusty old jeepster, too old to have ever been outfitted with it, was still giving good service in his daily traversing of the Aikens Ranch. It squeaked and rolled and shook all its occupants, but it still climbed out of every mud hole and ditch that it had been asked to.

Beach lost the odometer somewhere after its fourth rollover, but since the ranch is the only real estate this jeep will ever see again, it would probably be scrapped and buried wherever it took its last breath. The sweat was second nature to Beach, and he still considered his early morning rounds on the ranch as his most rewarding time of the day, a daily tradition begun by his father Jack McDade, many years ago. He could gaze at its unspoiled beauty, remember the good times with his family and day dream at will, which nourished his soul.

For the most part, his inspections were uneventful, but there was always the chance for the unexpected; a Florida Panther darting out from one of the large hammocks, a trophy boar grazing on the feed corn. It might be a Bald Eagle circling in high flight, with a scope on some innocent game. He would often find his cattle on the wrong side of the fence for a variety of reasons. Occasionally, it was the less desirable distraction, as in the two legged variety; cattle rustlers, hunters and poachers who had not 'checked in' and gotten permission from the caretaker; a group of teenagers on the hunt for good fresh cow patties, and the hallucinogenic mushrooms they yielded. The two legged animals always meant trouble. But he was the boss man, and the buck stopped with him.

Like a fisherman's gaze upon a constant blue ocean, McDade's scan took in every square foot of the thousands of acres of the Aiken Ranch. He knew the hardwoods by name, where the best hunting was, where the lodes of coquina rock lay subsurface waiting to be mined, if allowed. If there was something out of the ordinary, a color, a flash of light, a reflection it did not go unnoticed to Beach McDade. There were secrets only he knew from the days of his youth spent exploring with his father, the first foreman of the Aikens Ranch.

He hadn't really expected today to be one of those days as they were so close to beginning the first step of closing the deal on the sale of the ranch. It pleased him that a wealthy syndicate had plans to preserve the place for hunting leases and cattle farming. As far as Beach was concerned, it was the 'best case scenario' for the future of the ranch and its preservation. Although he maintained an active real estate license, he always considered himself more of a steward than a salesman.

He first noticed the light blue patch of color from a distance of 800 yards, and he was sure that its movement was independent of the light breeze in the air. He parked the jeep and grabbed the 30.06 from the window rack, and exited his ride. He laid the rifle over the roof of the cab and peered through the scope at his new target.

'Something keeping a low profile there...yup.' He could now see a man sitting on his ass looking through a pair of field glasses...now he was writing on a clipboard. Hmmm Beach said to himself as he considered his options. He could fire a few warning shots as was his custom, but this morning he was more curious than usual, 'let's see how close I can get to him before he sees me.'

Beach got back in the jeep, and drove to the opposite end of the hammock where the trespasser had taken his position. He felt he already knew the man's purpose as he was strategically situated near a creek that was integral in drainage and a good positive outfall. He parked the vehicle out of view and donned his snake boots. He was going to be wading in wetlands and swamps, and he didn't want any trouble from water moccasins or rattlers. He began his stalking from about 500 yards, through the edge of the cypress trees somewhat concealed in the shade. As he neared to within 100 or so yards, it became clear to him the nature of the man's mission. He would write on that clipboard, and then take another look through the binoculars, write a little more, and then it appeared as though he was talking into a headset, either recording or communicating via network cell phone.

'Perfect!' Beach thought to himself as he carefully, in stealth mode, made his final approach to the man who had his back to him. As he stood behind the visitor he leveled the barrel at his head noting that his shadow had overtaken his prey, and his presence would soon be detected. He could hardly keep from laughing.

The man was somewhat preoccupied gabbing away into his headset, until he looked down and away at McDade's silhouette, and the rifle. He instantly froze, and without turning, ever so slowly raised his arms over his head far as they would go. "Now, Mr.

McDade, don't shoot my ass! It was my idea to do this right, and get up with you, and get permission and all."

"Boy, you be on the wrong side of the fence, and if I was to put a bullet in your head, who could fault me with all the rustling been going on around here lately."

The man slowly turned around. "Beach, you know who I am, it's me Sammy, you know water management," the man spoke quivering, his face white as sheet.

"That right. You know I wouldn't have recognized you from a distance if I fired from a few hundred yards."

"Beach, Big Jim has got me by the balls, and you know what kind of man he is to work for. I got a wife and kids, I…"

"You tell that big son of a bitch, if he has things to deal with regarding this ranch he deals with me. I don't think our governor is apt to appoint someone who breaks the law while doing his job. If Big Jim wants to keep that Cush job, better have him call me before this thing really blows up in that dumb looking face of his. Pack your shit up and get out of here. I expect to be hearing from 'Big Jim' any day now. "

And he did the following morning.

* * * * * *

Throughout his thirty five year career in real estate and stewardship of the Aikens Ranch, Beach McDade had never considered fraternizing with the head of the Water Management Bureau. Unlike most landowners and managers, he kept his relations with the Bureau on the most minimalistic and honorable levels as possible. Beach preferred to feel the effects of its inspections, comments and Rulings, from as far a distance as he could justify. He was suspicious of any owner who cultivated the favor of the board with regard to comp plan amendments and other particular 'needs' that usually went against the grain of a clear and well defined Comprehensive Plan for Development. Didn't matter to Beach what Land Use or Zoning was involved, he regarded their actions as either politically or financially motivated, usually both. Beach viewed the Bureau's job as managing the state's waters for its citizens and not a speck more.

As the largest property owner in the State of Florida, the Bureau of Water Management was comprised entirely of governmentally appointed positions out of Tallahassee, ruling over an astronomical wealth in land holdings. In practice, there was minimal public monitoring of their internal workings, in a state that prided itself in its implementation of groundbreaking 'sunshine laws.'

The 'sugar fiasco' with all the suspect policies of federal price supports and other entitlements that had evolved along with the wayward projects of the Army Corps of Engineers reeked of political expediency. It was Beach's opinion that to win elections, you need only two things in Florida; money of course and more

37

money in the form of agricultural lobbies and the funds and endorsements they spin off. In its millennial transition, Florida had grown large enough in population and infrastructure to develop into a key state in national elections as well. Nouveau political leaders and benefactors, landowners and sugar barons could now claim their clout to be enshrined alongside 'Hizzoner' Mayor Richard Daley, the host emeritus of Chicago, and the canonized Don of the Democratic Party. The good 'ol boy network in Florida was alive and well.

So as he approached the beautiful glass and steel foyer of the Bureau's new Wellington office, Beach McDade remained in a guarded but curious state of anticipation. He had never met Jim McCravy in person, although he had spoken with him on numerous occasions regarding ranch issues, and had found him cooperative to a point. Nearly all his contact with the Bureau of Water Management had been with its field reps and technicians on clear tangible matters of drainage, water diversion rights, and any easements of interest in the developing of Florida lands.

When he got the phone call from the Bureau, it had been 'Big Jim' himself, the man. 'Why not stop down for a friendly visit and we'll do lunch'. Because of his fiduciary responsibility to the Aikens, and the impending contract for the sale of the ranch, he had little choice but to accept the invitation. McDade never doubted for a minute however, that Big Jim had some kind of bone he was going to pitch at him.

"Beach McDade for Mr. McCravy," the man announced as he entered the outer reception area.

"One moment, Sir," the comely redhead answered, "Mr. McDade is here Mr. McCravy." The reply was not to be shared, "He'll be just a few minutes, Mr. McDade, there's coffee and some Danish rolls over there, please help yourself," she urged as she returned her attention to other tasks.

Beach nodded his thanks and went over to pour himself a cup of joe. He figured he could use a little time to frame his thoughts. 'Don't talk too much as usual, wait on him. Don't start running your mouth, and throwing your opinions all around. You know he is going to come at you with some kind of deal. Listen.'

"Mr. McDade, Mr. McCravy is ready to see you now," she said getting up from her desk leading her charge into the penthouse suite. Beach was taken aback a little when the big man rose from his desk for he was even bigger than Beach had imagined from his pictures, "Glad to finally meet you, Beach, I've heard nothing but praise from the Aikens' people about how you take care of their little corner of paradise. The pleasure is certainly all mine."

Beach watched his hand disappear into the mammoth grip offered, "Beach…McDade, I have heard a great deal about you, too, sir," he replied with a show of eye contact. McDade then looked over to his right and offered his hand to a third man in the room, "Beach." And the man stood and thoroughly pumped his hand. "Adam."

Big Jim pushed his hands down in front of him like a seasoned politician subduing the crowd's applause while on the stump, "Let's get comfy, gentlemen," McCravy spoke as he lowered himself into his chair leaning all the way back in a gesture of informality. "Thanks for taking the time out, Beach, as I know you're very busy with this unreal market and all, but I felt compelled to meet with you in person. More importantly, I wanted to introduce you to Adam, and to bring you in on some exciting developments for our area. "Adam?"

"Go ahead Mr. McCravy, I'll defer for the time being."

"First, let me say that I am fully aware of all the developments with regard to the sale of the Aiken Ranch, who the

Buyers are, and when the Closing is scheduled and so forth. You are to be congratulated, Beach, your tireless efforts in keeping the ranch pristine, and brokering this deal, should be well rewarded and appreciated! Having said that, I can assure you there isn't any issue, at least at our end, that could derail the deal, but….for your interests and the Aikens' as well, you might consider taking a deep breath and re-examining things a bit."

"You signed off months ago, Mr. McCravy, are you going on record that the Bureau is prepared to renege on its comments and approvals with regard to the sale of the ranch?"

"No, no…nothing like that at all, Beach. Let me cut to the quick, sir, as you are a highly successful realtor, and will certainly understand these new developments once we've laid them out."

'Here comes the windup Beach thought.'

"Beach,…what we're seeing and hearing from the governor's office with regard to directives from both state and federal authorities on land management, is a rapidly transforming political landscape. It involves the rules and procedures for entitlement[s] citing specific reference to those properties outside the urban service boundaries, but within the Everglades Restoration Project. These directives also interface with any and all implementations of governmental projects and the environmental issues that may arise. Simply put, the government is going to require a certain level of dedicated acreage from the land owners for these projects, in return for all comp plan amendments, development rights and Land Use intensity granted to those property owners. Follow me so far, Beach?"

"Go ahead I'm listening."

"While these requirements can't directly interfere with your selling the ranch, they can affect the future value of the ranch to your Buyers, and they may well limit access to some of the most desirable areas for hunting and such ... I understand your Buyers are a Midwest syndicate interested in co-ownership and hunting leases, etc.... that correct?"

"That would be the interest for the near term, yes."

"So, while this won't prohibit the sale of the ranch, it will have to be disclosed to the Buyers, and there will definitely be some significant soft costs involved, apart from any possible future eminent domain procedures on behalf of the state. You know, Beach, there is an awful lot of talk about phosphates, sugar and water releases from the locks these days, directly stemming from managing the big lake. People are hearing how phosphates and excess nutrients create algae blooms and kill sea grasses, it has become a hot issue. 'Where does it come from they ask. Don't back pump sugar's water into the lake, they say. Stop polluted releases into our estuaries, send it south. It's a political firestorm, Beach. It's-"

"You're preaching to the choir, Mr. McCravy. Phosphates and algae blooms have always been a part of Florida's history at one time or another; nothing new under the sun there, sir.

"Well said, Beach. You and I as natives understand that all too well, but the general public is clearly being given a different perspective through the media. Agreed?"

"The media will always take care of its side of the street first, Mr. McCravy, and then your side as well. The McCravy family, as well as the McDades, have a long connection with the land in and around Lake Okeechobee, and there is one thing that we both should definitely agree on. You don't manage or alter what is, by original design, a cistern. In its creation, when the sea levels dropped and created what is now Okeechobee, everything left for its perfect management was already in place. By original design, it was an amazing system that regularly, and quite perfectly I might add, outflowed excess water to the sheet plain of the Everglades for percolation and water storage. You and your cronies from Tallahassee and DC, though only inheriting a portion of this mess, have wrought unbelievable damage to the big lake and virtually all of south Florida's main estuaries for the last seventy years. Really Big Jim, why bring me in on all this diversionary rhetoric? You should be talking to the sugar people who receive all the price supports and fuel the money pipeline gushing out to Washington. Phosphates have been in Florida ever since the dinosaurs, Mr. McCravy; in Florida Bay, Lake Okeechobee, Ft Meyers, it occurs naturally. As for the spiking high levels in Lake Okeechobee, you can thank your imbecilic friends over at the Army Corps for that. They were wrong to attempt to straighten the Kissimmee River to begin with, and anyone with a polyp brain knew it would interfere with natural filtration and flow and eventually kill the river. And then when they started working on the project, they were advised not to burrow deeper than twenty feet at the mouth of the river where it enters the lake, but the idiots did. Now they have unearthed probably the largest phosphate lode in the state into the effluence of the big lake. And, to complete their mission of destruction, they spent even more money to rework the river back to the way the good Lord made her. Riparian rights trampled, the Corps committed a homicide on the Kissimmee proving once again they are more of a political kick in the ass than an institution of engineering science!"

A good deal of dead air

"You're certainly entitled to your opinions, Beach, but we're getting off task here."

'He's right' Beach thought,' you've already lost it. Shut up and listen.'

"Why have you summoned me here, Mr. McCravy and what is…I'm sorry, sir, what was your name?"

"Adam, Adam Wendt."

"What is Adam's role in all of this? Could you possibly be running for office, Mr. Wendt, or are you just running some kind of interference on behalf of the Mott dynasty?"

Having done his homework, Wendt reacted with a chuckle, "No worries, Beach, nothing as sinister as that."

"Mr. Wendt brings a great deal of expertise and notoriety to the table; in fact I'm surprised you haven't caught him on TV, Beach. He has a solution that could mean a great deal more money for the Aikens, one that would be reflected, of course, in commissions due regarding the sale of the ranch. The contracted selling price is 94 million dollars is it not?"

Play along, Beach, "It is."

"Adam and his people believe the Aikens' property is the key to the future of Martin, St. Lucie and Palm Beach counties. With the tech backing he brings to the table, he and his team will be able to navigate through this mess, establish a great bio-tech research facility into the area, gaining further entitlements by dedicating the premium upland portions of the ranch to the people. That would seem to be in conflict with your Buyers' vision for the ranch."

"You're saying returning some of the premium lands to the people, Big Jim, which translated means turning the whole place into a giant toilet. You know you're going to need a humongous rebuilt dike to monkey with, also at taxpayers' expense, and they're already picking up the tab for all the bribes being handed around here like political flyers. Silence, exhale and pause…'play along, you're getting a little off center,' "How am I to undo and void the Contract with my Buyers?"

"Oh well…" McCravy shifted his gaze down and away and began inspecting his fingernails, "once they've received these disclosures, and have done the math and reevaluated their projections, they will be content to look elsewhere. I'm quite sure they are astute businessmen, and they will eventually realize the diminishing return on their investment over time."

"Jim, if I might," Adam interjected, "Beach, on behalf of my partners in California, I am prepared to present you with an offer in the tidy sum of 120 million dollars for the Aikens Ranch. Along with that a 3% commission headed your way, no other brokers; I am speaking as the Principal. Our investment group has established and maintained a very strong and respected developmental presence in Orlando for decades; you can check us out to your complete satisfaction. What are your thoughts?"

"If what you gentlemen say is true and accurate, and it most certainly will be thoroughly reviewed; it might not sit well with the Buyers. It could be viewed as a tardy disclosure, and cause for a Cancelling of the Contract. I could be seen as doing a disservice to the Buyers and failing to perform my agency duties to the Aikens," Beach mused. "In either case, I want data and information from you, Mr. Wendt; any preliminary work to date, something I can review and go to all parties with. I'll at least require a preliminary site plan, boundary survey and wetland delineation, and all comments from the state as they roll in. I need to see what kind of footprint you're going to leave behind."

"Not a problem, Beach, I will give you everything my land planners have at this time, and all developments, comments and rulings as they come in," Wendt assured enthusiastically.

"I'd like all your stuff too, Mr. McCravy."

"Consider it done, Beach. How did you know that some of this horizontal work had already been in the pipeline?"

"Surely you must be kidding, Big Jim. All right then, here's my card gentlemen, I'll get working on it when I receive the material. Good day, I'll just let myself out." Beach rose, shook hands with the pair, and made his escape.

'How I love it when leaders of men figure me as a stupid cracker,' Beach thought to himself as he hit the fresh air. 'It really makes all this bullshit a lot more fun.'

* * * * * *

The high pitched tin roof straight lined down, shielding the western side of the cabin's entrance and front porch from all but the latest of afternoon sun. Sunsets here were the kind of photoshoots many magazines pay a lot of money for. No green flash, just a visual symphony of light and hue, water and swamp, flourishing wildlife and the sounds of dusk competing with a silence so dedicated, you could hear the blood coursing through your ears.

Louis spent every late afternoon right there rocking on that porch to clear his head and bare his heart to his Redeemer. It didn't take long to dismiss all the babbling of the world, and he found that he could easily distance himself from the pressures and forces of evil that were coming at him on a daily basis. If his thoughts and plans did not square with his maker, he could certainly not hide from the revelations living all around him. As always his devotions delivered to him the answers and assurance he was seeking, along with that peaceful Spirit dwelling deep within his soul.

The old captain laid his Bible on a small table along with his readers, replacing them with his sunglasses giving the panorama an even richer saturation of color, if that were possible. This particular human perspective was his alone, witnessed from the only residence in sight, save for one trophy house recently constructed at the western border of the swamp. He chuckled to himself as he considered the contrast between the two homes, wondering what could possibly be going through the mind of a man who erected such a concrete eyesore right on top of such a magnificent still life. Louis considered and saw that his personal salvation had him looking ahead, and the rich man's display of wealth had required him always to look back.

"Another beauty of an evening eh, Louis, something else."

"Afternoon, Billy. Take a load off, I'll grab a couple of beers."

"Don't mind if I do, cap," Replied McDade as he eased into the rocker on the other side of the table. Louis emerged from the screen door with a couple of long necks and passed one over to Bill.

"Thank you, sir. Come down here a lot, but this 'bout as far as I get. Just like to end the day here."

Informalities over, the two old friends shared the silence and a view of the world not readily available to nor sought after by many folks anymore. They valued their unshakeable bond of friendship, the fruit of their many days helping out one another in times of trouble. Then there were those incredibly good times spent fishing and hunting that only sportsmen cherish above all else. Louis did have a hand in the building of this cabin just as Bill McDade helped Louis construct his cracker house not far from the water a few miles to the southeast. They both knew the value and joy in the life they had shared, and neither felt inclined at the moment to revisit any of those numerous adventures therein. For right now, it was the end of the day, a moment to take in, and not work the head.

Silence was golden as the two gazed at the fading light of late afternoon as it temporarily retreated behind the broken high cirrus clouds of an early fall cool front. Brilliant golds and oranges slowly giving way to pinks and indigos before the sinking and cooling air finally dissolved the clouds of dusk into a final fiery 'good evening.' Louis got up to light the hurricane lantern, adjusted the wick and returned to his rocker. Evening was now upon these old friends as they waited in silence for the overture of the sounds of swamp life in the darkness.

"Billy, what you have done for me and Cami here…I am beyond grateful…you have given us a piece of heaven on earth, a needed refuge. I pray that someday I can return the favor old friend. But... there are things you need to know-"

"Louis, I'm quite sure that I already know more than you think."

"Probably do, Bill, yet it wasn't all covered in the press. There are some serious issues and unfinished business that Cami and I have yet to deal with."

McDade broke into a genuine laughter in an attempt to deflect Louis' somber tone, "Louie, how long have you and I lived in this tropical jungle, I mean were the truth be known, we have seen them all come and go haven't we; you by water, me standing by on shore. A couple of old crackers once knee deep in trouble, but now finding deliverance in the form of beauty and contentment. The carpetbaggers, the real estate shysters and legal shills, pilots and captains, drug smugglers and pirates, white hats, black hats, the ultimate vermin in gray hats, are there any characters we haven't come across?

More laughter.

"That mining operation that was taking fill out yonder for a while, you remember how hard I fought it? That mouthpiece for the 'applicant' owned a fleet of trucks on standby as he waited for the county to rule in his favor. Well, he had a good thing going until the ram on one of the hoppers jammed. The driver was caught slicing up square groupers from the bottom layer in the bin, scattering them all over the high ground up there to the northwest. Somehow, it never went to trial, but it did make the back page of the paper. That lawyer became pretty prominent in St Lucie County, especially when the packages got smaller and smaller."

McDade pressed on, "What about that pilot buddy of yours

that could fly everything from a crop duster to a 747 and everything in between, even choppers. When they recovered that King Air that nosedived into the ocean, they ruled it 'pilot error,' even though everyone around here pretty much knew the fuel lock had been toyed with. No, Louis, you don't have to fill in too many blanks for this old man. I got a pretty good idea what you and that pretty gal of yours have been left to deal with regarding this latest episode. By the way, do you realize how lucky you are to have that to come home to?"

"Not a day goes by." McDade took a long pull of his beer and set it down before starting to rub his forehead and eyes in an attempt to frame his thoughts.

"I'm glad you took me up on staying here, Louie, I've wanted to go over some things, things that have been dogging me for a long, long time. You're, well...you're like the son I lost, a tad older, but that's how I feel. I couldn't be happier for you, she's special. I know she can't replace your first wife, but she sure can stand alongside her." With that McDade eased back against the rocker and downed the remainder of his beer. His eyes moved off Louis into the night, and he was quiet once more. Louis could not help but feel the can opening effect of McDade's words, although the old captain suspected they were projections of what was really weighing on his friends mind. From experience, he sensed a stirring in the man's heart, and Louis knew that a release was building deep within the soul of his good friend. In a matter of moments, the tears began to flow as McDade buried his head into his hands.

Louis remained quiet as he walked alongside him from the chair, letting those years of grief over the loss of his son finally find their way out of a softened heart. As the tears soon gave way to sobbing wail, Louis got up and placed his hand on Billy's shoulder to give comfort and assurance that they were together on this.

Louis said nothing for he knew this was a necessary and positive exorcism where words would just be a hindrance. The two remained that way for quite a while.

"Look at me, Louie, bawling like a little kid. Sorry to dampen your evening."

"Hah...are you kidding me! I am too glad to be here right now, and the main reason I'm here has been made perfectly clear to me." 'Haven't got it all dialed in yet,' Louis thought to himself, 'Lord help me to be honest.'

"You see, Billy… I have been down this dark and twisting road that you are trying to get off of. I spent all those years after her death hating that asshole that drove into her. I lived in constant bitterness, hating life, hating God, hating drunks…even hating the sea because it no longer provided this ingrate an escape from the sadness and loneliness following her death. I was regressing back into the days of my rebellious youth. I deserted my own daughter staying away for months on end, letting her find her own way with my sister. What a wretch. I'm amazed the good Lord kept me alive long enough so as to make my peace with Him. Hard hearts and stiff necks are not subject to change very easily. A heart like mine had to be pretty much crushed to take me to the bottom. When I finally got there, in that totally dark hole that I had dug for myself, I struggled often to keep from sticking a gun in my mouth. By my calculations, I was completely and finally alone in the world. Or so I thought."

"Here," Louis grabbed his Bible and put it in McDade's left hand, "no strings, no pressure, and no worries. When you have the time, crack it open once in a while, there is no one way to read it. I pray you hear that voice as I did, back when I needed it the most. It is a greater, sovereign outside voice of peace and understanding, and it lives. For a fool like me it was the beginning of true wisdom.

Go ahead, take it now and read this tonight while our fellowship remains fresh."

"Louie...I never was much of a..."

"Take it my friend, and know this. You are not alone tonight, you have never truly been alone, and will never be alone in all your days in this life. Check it out, Billy, and please drop by in the morning. Hold on..." Louis placed the bookmark somewhere within the book's many pages. "You might as well start here," Louis gave it back to his friend and went inside the cabin for the night.

A knock on the door had Louis jumping out of bed in his traditional night garb of t shirt and skivvies. His host was standing on the front porch looking out over Lake Eden and beyond, tapping the book his guest had given him the night before. As Louis opened the screen door, Bill McDade walked right by him and took a seat at the simple kitchen table in the main room.

"Louis, I want to thank you for being my friend, and for always being there. I read where you bookmarked the passages for me, and...well... it did give me a sense of peace. I could see where the words were true and honest, and that they were, in fact, painting a very clear picture of me and my condition."

Louis smiled as he nodded his head, 'Pretty amazing message isn't it, Bill?"

McDade looked down at the worn Bible before responding, "The old man used to drag Beach and I to church once in a while, but it didn't stick you know, it all seemed kind of mechanical rather than personal. I never had a Bible; no one ever spoke much about it around here either. I always believed in the golden rule as I lived out my life; that abiding by it would forever let me solve all my problems, however dire. But last night, the moment I cracked it open even before reading the first word….hard to explain…. this feeling of warmth came over me. It was like something unseen massaging my heart."

"Tell it my friend", a smiling Louis encouraged, "the Lord has drawn you to Him and has given you eyes that see and ears that hear! Your heart is at peace and now receives an understanding in the deepest part of your being; for the Spirit has begun to take up residence in your soul. "

Bill tried to hand the Bible back to Louis but Louis stopped him in his tracks, "This is my gift to you. It will always remind you of this time and place and what we have shared together here. I have plenty of Bibles, and I want you to have this one at your side at all times. Try and go into it every day even if it's only a few minutes; for this is the beginning of true wisdom which will be a comfort to you forever. Now, finally, we'll have something other than fishing and hunting to talk about." Both men broke out in laughter.

"By the way, Billy, what has your brother Beach been up to, is he still running that big ranch out west?"

"Yeah he is, Louis, taking up a lot of his time these days as the whole place is being bought out by a hunting group up north from Chicago. Talked to him last week and it appears there might be a few last minute hiccups in the deal."

"Oh?

"Something to do with the Everglades restoration …government guidelines or development changes in the law, don't really know that much about it. You'd have to ask him he's the real estate guru in the family. There is also some side door interest in the property from a group from California with ties to Mickey World up in Orlando. Some guy named Adam….whatever, came in with a higher offer as a backup."

Louis' joy of the early morning was suddenly being siphoned off with the mere mention of the man's name, "Billy, I don't suppose that man would be Adam Wendt would it?"

"Hmmm…sounds familiar, come to think of it, Louis, I do believe you might be right; Adam Wendt… that's it. Beach spent the morning down there at Water Management and he was the guy that sat in on the meeting. Beach said he didn't say much, but that he was friendly and he obviously was representing a very wealthy group of investors."

"Well, Billy my friend, it's time we finished our conversation."

                              * * * * * *

Big Jim pressed his intercom and hailed his administrative aide, "Caroline, has Mr. McDade left the office?"

"Yes he has Mr. McCravy, he poured a coffee refill and left about ten minutes ago."

"Very good, Caroline, it's been a really long week, why don't you just take the rest of the day off. I have some afternoon appointments in Palm Beach, and there's nothing pressing around here that needs our attention. Have fun, sweetie."

"Why thank you so much, Mr. McCravy, that's very considerate of you."

"Happy to do it, see you on Monday. Bye." After waiting about ten minutes, Big Jim walked into the reception area to find the remainder of his staff either gone or out for lunch. Satisfied he and Wendt were the only two in the office; he locked the main door and shut off his aide's intercom before returning to his private board room.

Big Jim reached into his desk drawer once again to pour himself a belt of bourbon, "Can I get you anything, Adam, bourbon, scotch, a brewski?"

"I'm fine Jim, really. So...where do you think we stand at this point?"

"Adam, I've pushed this about as far as I can go. If you have been paying attention, I think you would admit that we have taken a lot of the steam out of this deal, and this should begin the unravelling of this Contract going hard. These Chicago guys have done their share of due diligence, and even paid 90,000 for a 60 day extension. They have worked hard on the numbers and in my professional opinion and experience in these matters, they will not go hard on the Contract come January tenth."

"You're sure Mr. McCravy."

"I'm sure. I can read people pretty damn well just like I can read you, Mr. Wendt."

"Oh?"

"Hunting is a great pastime, don't you agree, Adam? Big Jim paused to suppress a laugh that might take him off task. "Anyway, these guys aren't quite as deep in the pockets as your gang, and the 'adjusted' return and carry on this piece is not going to convince them to go forward."

The big guy looked down for a moment before leaning forward going eyeball to eyeball with his guest as he rested his chin on the palm of his right hand atop the huge desk, "Hear this well, Adam. I know all there is to know about you and your Cal buddies, how you have conducted your business in Kissimmee and Orlando, and even in the Bahamas. I even know how much you personally risked in positioning yourself as lead dog in this deal, and the level of wealth that came with it. I don't really care about any of the particulars; I say these things simply to make a point, and insure that I will be compensated as we have previously agreed. You see, Adam, you come to this table weighted down with significant baggage; should you be squeezed into a compromising situation down the line, legal or otherwise, the buck will have to stop with you. Putting it another way… you go against the grain and start rocking the boat, you and this project will cease to exist."

"Whoa, Jim, where are you going with this? Getting a bit heavy around here aren't we. What kind of man do you take me for?"

Big Jim now broke out in his familiar guttural laugh, "What do I take you for? Hah…most likely as a man who would have no problem in taking someone out. That's what I take you for Mr. Motivational speaker!"

"I have never killed anybody in my entire life!"

"Fine, Adam, you want to mince words, your privilege, but as I have already said, I don't care! I really don't care. When 12:01 January eleventh arrives if I were you, I would move fast and take control of the property. Once you and your people go hard on the Contract, you will pay my fee, the agreed upon number in the manner that you and I have already laid out. We're not waiting for comp plan changes, final site plan approval from the counties, no extensions, no accelerator clauses, and we're certainly not going to wait on the state to rule on your DRI. So, there it is, then. When you go hard and take control of the property that is the precise moment that you will be finishing up with me. I do hope I've made myself perfectly clear."

"Yes, Mr. McCravy, indeed you have," a somewhat subdued Adam Wendt replied.

"Splendid, Adam," Big Jim smiled back as he made a return to informality. "Now as I have said, I have taken this deal about as far I can drive it. You have one more screen test to go through, however."

"And that would be?"

"You and I have been invited for lunch tomorrow at Henrique Flores' house in Palm Beach. I assume I can expect you to attend."

"Flores? I don't believe that we have ever met."

"Well then, it's about time you met your new neighbor, Adam. You would be wise to do a little homework before noon tomorrow. Meet me here and my chauffeur will drive us."

"Are we through, Jim?"

"We are through."

* * * * * *

Palm Beach has always existed as a global winter conclave for the elite to gather, play and network with one another. Whether from old money, new money, political prominence or celebrity fame, a residence on this island always provided an acceptable cachet of social rank for its residents.

Traditions still remain in the form of Royal Palm avenues, highly selective retailers, impeccably detailed landscaping with bordered privacy walls of high hedgerows. Tile roofs, exquisitely crafted windows, balconies, pools and fountains still showcase classic homes of block and stucco incorporating Mediterranean, European and Colonial architectural themes. Exclusive marinas abound, providing easy private access to the numerous mega yachts, international class motor sailors and custom sport fishing boats the Palm Beachers were known to amass; whether they spent much time on them or not. If it was horses and polo ponies there was the equine community of Wellington west of town.

The modern era of new money and overnight tech billionaires had been slowly redefining the look of the town in recent years, with knockdowns of old, stately 'winter cottages' morphing into double wide concrete castles with custom formed turrets and spires. More and more, lot lines that once held grass and lawns, were discarded for the near zero lot lines these trophy homes required. Tastes were changing.

As the limo pulled into the manned, gated oceanfront mansion of Henrique Flores in Manalapan towards the southern end of the island, Adam Wendt was going over his mental outline regarding the history of the Flores family both in Cuba and Florida.

Wendt had actually undertaken a thorough study of the two families comprising the sugar dynasties of south Florida, at the very beginning of his quest to bring the tech sector into the area. He reminded himself to be friendly, but understated, curious but detached, accommodating but not easily bullied. Balance was the key here; it was the Flores' backyard for the time being.

There were more than a few men walking the grounds upon their arrival, but they were watchful and careful in maintaining their distance from the guests in part due to their training; perhaps on account of recognizing McCravy's limo as it entered the compound.

"Hola, Mr. McCravy, please come in, Mr. Flores will be with you soon. He is on phone to Washington, and will be a few moments. Sir, you would be Mr. Wendt and he is so looking forward to meeting with you. Please…," instructed the Cuban beauty as she outstretched her arm to point them in the direction of Flores' man cave off the large foyer. "He will be with you shortly, can I get either of you something to drink, water, juice, or perhaps a rum and grapefruit?"

"That sounds wonderful, Rosa, and one for Mr. Wendt as well," Big Jim replied with a smile as he nodded towards Wendt.

"Certainly, Mr. McCravy," she answered as she closed the double doors.

"Take a look around, Adam. I think you'll find that Flores has been around the block more than a few times."

Adam had already begun the tour, however, and was pouring over all the pictures of Flores with many politicians to include a few Presidents. There were candid shots of Flores at play, standing by big fish, golfing with PGA pros, wearing an Atlanta Braves team jacket with ballplayers at spring training. He moved on to the trophy case and the many figures of sailfish and marlin, along with tagging rewards and citations from the International Game Fishing Association, on whose Board of Directors Flores held a seat. In the trophy case there was a picture of Flores and his father with Ernest Hemingway in Havana. His study tour was then interrupted by the sounds of squeaky rubber boat shoes as they gripped the polished marble floor.

"How are you, Big Jim? Good to see you once again, my friend." Henrique Flores bellowed as he burst through the double doors. He went right to McCravy taking his hand and half hugging the man in the gesture that has become commonplace in media events. "And you must be Adam, so pleased to meet you," he added as he grabbed Wendt's extended hand with a firm grip and rigid eye contact as he placed his left hand on his guest's shoulder." Welcome to our little corner of the world. Please, sit down and relax."

Rosa distributed the cocktails to all before leaving and closing the doors.

"I hope you approve, it is our family's private reserve with fresh squeezed ruby red from our groves."

"Absolutely… the best ever, Henrique," toasted Wendt.

"Please call me Henry, Adam."

"Henry, the best rum and grapefruit I've ever sipped!" Adam let the chuckle linger and took a quick snapshot of the icon who sat across from him. Flores was a handsome man of sixty or so Wendt guessed, impeccably groomed with a lot of mousse and a trimmed moustache on a deeply tanned face. Clad in black pants, Sperry topsiders and a loose embroidered white shirt, Flores certainly fit the part of his larger than life reputation. There was hardly a trace of an accent as he spoke near perfect English. "I must say your impressive fishing achievements and dedication to the sport are admirable. I am in awe, as I too love to fish the blue water."

"Thank you so much. Then it is my desire to have you join us this January at the Sailfish Club, and fish the Gold Cup with us as an angler. It is a fun tournament, and I hear you are an experienced angler in your own right."

"Kind words, Henry, but I think I have a lot to learn."

"Adam, when it comes to fish, I think we all have a great deal to learn. No matter how experienced one thinks he has become, there is a fish swimming in the sea ready to make a fool of him," Flores stated as he broke out in laughter throwing his guests a wink. "Such a beautiful winter day, I think we'll have lunch outside."

Flores directed his guests through the adjoining living room and led them out through a pair of huge sliding glass doors, activated by pneumatic ram and a pedal switch mounted on the floor in the corner of the gateway to the outside patio. An elegant table had been prepared on the custom marble tile providing a spectacular view of the ocean; Mar-a-Lago and the Kennedy compound had nothing to compare with it.

Flores took his seat at the head of the table directing his two guests to seats on either side of him where a fresh round of drinks had been set for the three. Flores rubbed his hands together and took a fairly large sip as he stared out at the aquamarine and indigo water. He kept his eyes riveted offshore at a trio of sport fishing boats situated on the well-defined line where the water color went from turquoise to an indigo blue, maintaining silence as he preferred his guests to steer the conversation.

"Stunning, Henry, you certainly possess a beautiful still life of land and sea. Those boats can't be more than a couple of miles off the beach, are they apt to get sailfish in that close," a curious Wendt asked in order to prick the dead air.

"They should, Adam, the conditions today are near perfect;

clean water, a well-defined color change in combination with an equally sharp current edge. Their kites are up, the goggle eyes are tearing up the surface, it is only a manner of time before the sails find them. From here to Deerfield Beach, the Gulf Stream generally runs closer to shore, than at any other point between the Yucatan and all of Florida, and today we can have a box seat even if we cannot play. We can hope for such conditions when we fish the tournament."

"What are the dates for the event, Henry?"

"January 12-16th."

"Oh no, I fear I might be tied down with the business contracting for the property; I certainly hope that is not the case."

"No problem, Adam, if there is a conflict we'll just try for the Buccaneer the week after. The fish should be around, and I completely applaud you for your devotion to this project."

"Adam and I have been working long and hard on this one." interjected Big Jim in order to remind both men of his implied pivot man status, "We want to see a project of this magnitude go forward on the northeast side of the lake. It's a win-win for us all." The three men all nodded and toasted the sentiment.

Flores was thinking it might be time for dropping the bait back a bit, "I think it's wonderful that you want to bring such a world class research community into our neighborhood, Adam. It will bring jobs, tax revenues and of course a great deal of media attention. I like that part of it the most because they will be knocking down your door and looking over your shoulders instead of mine all of the time." A laugh was shared. "It is not enough that my brother and I provide thousands of jobs, tax revenues and an expansive 'green' business to the lake area. The media and environmental watchdogs are like a swarm of mosquitos, and I'll be quite happy to let you and your partners swat them for a while."

"I saw a little of that while working this project through with Jim, and you certainly have my sympathies, Henry."

"And what did you learn, Adam?"

"I would say that I, also have been down this road in the past," Adam paused taking a quick glance at McCravy who imperceptibly rolled his eyes, "in Orlando and the Bahamas of late. When you set your dreams into motion, when you follow through on the best of your efforts, there will always be those who don't share your visions. Progress always comes with a price, and it is usually paid for by those who have the least to gain. In the face of all that, I think you should be congratulated for how well you have managed the status quo all these years. 'Whatever it takes' is a credo I have long believed in." Satisfied with his diplomacy Wendt again looked over at Big Jim who by now was rattling his silverware looking down at his cellphone.

"Very interesting, Adam. I am not unfamiliar with your teachings; in fact I made it a point to review a couple of your books. I have no problem with the worship of self enhancement and performance or the desire for the comforts of life, but I am a man old enough and wise enough to know where and when to draw the line in this kind of 'I-Thou' world view. There are things I cannot do or get entirely done on my own, and I must rely on others to do them for me."

"I quite agree whole heartedly, Henry. As for me,-"

"I hate politics and politicians in general, even though over the years, I have at times required from them a great deal of 'civil' support. Whatever the cost, on either side of the aisle, I have chosen to fund it, so as to never ever let myself be in their debt. My family has for generations been farmers, wealthy farmers, yes, but we have no interest in getting involved with the power brokers and prostitutes in Tallahassee and Washington. We are content to let them wage war amongst themselves, for that is their lot in life and the key to their survival. They have been playing around with the lake water, digging canals here and there for 120 years. Unfortunately, the killer 'canes of the 1920's changed everything for the lake. I see my family as latecomers who saw nothing but the outstretched palms of too many politicians and land owners. As neighbors Mr. Wendt, you and I will need to focus on our individual needs, of course. Equally, important, however, we must both be completely aware of the needs of the other. Yes?"

"Most certainly, Henry, I appreciate your candor. Why then, is the media so wrapped up in all that's going on around the lake? It seems a lot of hyperbole is being thrown at what is a normal, evolutionary requirement in the lake's development." Wendt suddenly became aware of a very large shoe pressing hard on his foot from across the table out of the view of his host. He had no problem processing Big Jim's pierced eyes.

"Well, Adam…as you have said, in every great period of growth, there will always be a percentage of the people who are going to have to give up something. Those very people want land from me to mitigate the damage that has been around for a long time. When my family first set up shop, most of the lake's hydrology was already set into place. I am only utilizing those engineering constraints to my best advantage. I did not put them there. Once in a while, during times of unusually heavy rainfall, the dike must be protected with massive water releases within the lock structures east and west. I do see that it hurts the rivers, especially the Indian River Lagoon. I love to fish, and I cherish those days spent going for trout and snook up there. I might compromise in some way, but the 'people' are not my Buyers, politicians and governments are the ones across the table from me. The people even voted to make a down payment, and please observe, Adam, who is really dragging their feet on such a purchase. I think deeding a portion of my land for the purpose of allowing water to return to a southerly flow into the Everglades sheet plain could be a good compromise. I can pull and back pump water just as easily from a flow through canal as I can from the lake, and nutrient excesses are headed towards the right place to be 'scrubbed' so to speak. I would feel better about the overflow going where it is needed, and we could definitely curtail some of the heavy discharges into the estuaries. Personally, I would welcome a constant safety valve controlling lake levels rather than the lock and flood gate extremes the Army Corps gambles with today. Then again, very little attention is being given to you and your partners in Orlando and Kissimmee, and how they have contributed to the lake's phosphate and nutrient imbalance over the years. Not to throw you a jab, Mr. Wendt, but given the immensity of your holdings and their profitability, how much media attention are you receiving regarding your engineering and how it has impacted the environment. Just remember what I said about debt, and know that I am not in their debt; nearly to the extent that they might be in mine. They were the ones who made bribes legal with their Pac and super Pac practices. You will do well to let them be and not force their hand, for they have enough troubles of their own. We live here and we need to pay close attention to one another's needs. Ok."

"Henry, those are strong words to live by." The pressure on his foot ceased.

"Then let us drink to this new friendship," toasted Flores with a sure nod of the head. Flores hit the call button under the table to summon his stewardess, "I'm hungry for some lobster salad, Rosa and another drink for us all, thank you."

* * * * * *

Cami was in the process of just finishing the breakfast cleanup when the knock on the screen door took Louis away from the penning of a letter to his daughter, "Louis, Bill."

"Come on in, you just missed a fine breakfast of speckie perch and eggs."

"Dang sure beat my tough old bagel and peanut butter. Louis, after much consideration of our discussion a while back, I called Beach yesterday, and filled him in on everything you've told me regarding the piracy and killing," replied Bill McDade as he took a seat at the table.

"I got no problem with that, Billy, we're all family. How about some coffee?"

"Sounds good, I'll have some."

"I'm kind of glad you did call him, because whether he likes it or not, he has inherited at least a partial involvement in this mess. Guys like Wendt have a quality about them that seems to naturally involve people like flypaper; the more you try to extricate yourself from it, the stickier everything becomes. Beach should know everything we do, what we know now and might learn later. We love his honesty, for he's man who is not afraid to speak his mind. However, as heartfelt as he has been about the environment and its continual degradation over the years, I worry that he might go too far in resisting or maybe undermining this play for the ranch by Wendt. It's unfortunate, but he definitely needs to be on his guard."

"You know Beachie, Louis, he wasn't born yesterday. In fact, the first thing that came out of his mouth had everything to do with what you just said."

65

"Louie is right, Bill, this man Wendt is pure evil and he has all the connections to see that his plans aren't compromised in any way," chimed in Cami as she topped off the two men's coffee. "You can probably count on him retaining that disgusting Teflon exterior as well; he has plenty of others, male and female, to do his bidding."

"I appreciate both of your concerns I…pretty much relayed all of this to Beach so I was kind of taken back with his reaction."

"He is going to be on his guard isn't he?"

"Of course, Louis, but over the phone he sounded like he was enjoying every minute of the progression of this deal; the meeting with Water Management, the side door manipulations, the role of big sugar; he referred to it as the best damn soap opera a man of his years could ever hope to get caught up in."

"That's exactly what worries me, Billy," Louis lamented, "He spends a lot of time alone out at that huge ranch, and it wouldn't be hard for him to be the victim of some kind of accident."

"Yeah, I hear you. I said the same thing to him and you know what his response was," McDade stated as he arose now pleading with his hands, "That he was needed and a necessary instrument in Wendt's plans. As long as the deal was alive, he would be alive. After that... well, I'll cross that bridge when I come to it; vintage Beach McDade."

"Are we surprised," confessed Louis as he slowly shook his head, trying to find a direction to take this discussion.

"What is today, Louis, December 28th or something?"

"29th."

"Okay. Beach wants us to meet him out at the ranch right after New Year's, and he'll be able to explain more of all this in much greater detail. He said he needed more time to sift through all the 'due diligence' that was pouring in on a regular basis, but that it was extremely important that the three of us meet out there."

"Alright, Billy, done. Monday sound good to you?"

"That'll work," nodded McDade as he shook Louis' hand and gave Cami a big hug. And out the door he went.

"This is not working out like I had hoped, Cami, getting the McDades all wrapped up in this crap. It doesn't seem like it's going to wind itself down on its own either. All I wanted to do was to go catch a fish, make a little jingle to set my girl up in school, and look at the mess I got us all in now."

"Hey, if you hadn't taken Frank up on his offer, you wouldn't be sitting at my breakfast table looking at your beautiful soon to be wife either. Look, Captain," Cami added as she came over and sat on Louis' lap, "we're in this together, and we will know what to do when the time comes. I have complete faith in our abilities," she stated as she picked up his left hand, placing it on her magnificent breast as she initiated a long and tender kiss.

"You slam me every time, darlin', I am defenseless in every way," was all Louis could say as she took him by the hand and led him into the bedroom.

* * * * * *

"Hello, Louis, what do you got to say for yourself, tell me something good."

"Not a whole lot, Crafty, still laying low up here in the savannas enjoying life with the sweetie. We're just trying to take it a day at a time and enjoy the day. Heard you had a good season in the Azores, that is until you quickly bolted out of there. Mikey called me at your instruction and pretty much filled me in. I'm glad you called, Crafty, it was time we checked in and got caught up on things. Tell me how it all played out over there."

"Yeah… our asshole buddy Wendt sent a point man to come fish with us, so I concocted a story to make that happen. It gave me a little time to have Freddie mix him up a land based ciguatera long island tea disguised as a double 12 yr. old Scotch. I'll bet that long plane ride home was one to remember."

"Haven't lost your touch, Crafty, and that's a good thing because I'm feeling we are about to jump back in the fray."

"How's that, Louie?"

"Wendt has resurfaced in Palm Beach, and it seems that he is been hanging out with the likes of Henrique Flores and some fairly big hitters out of Orlando and Tallahassee. Apparently he has designs on buying the Aikens' Ranch on behalf of his California syndicate to add to their Florida dynasty. From what I've learned in the news, the master plan would call for a world class research park and it has certainly attracted a lot of attention. Anyway, he is around and kicking up his heels, and we both know that means trouble."

"Sorry to hear that, cap, but I never did figure him to stray far from Florida. I guess you probably heard I'm fishing out of Sailfish Marina this winter with Emory and the Greek, nothing too heavy just a few days and the Buc tournament so far. At least I have a bunk where I can be out of commission and out of sight or whatever comes first. Damn, Louis, I for one am burnt out on trying to lose this dickhead and anyone else that he sends to do me. Lately, I have been thinking about taking a different course to deal with this situation. Maybe we can kind of flush him out, you know, not like it went down in Cuba, but in a far more public way. Somehow we have to tie him to the deed, catch him with his hand in the cookie jar."

"I'll think on that, Crafty, but for the present keep a very low profile will you. I have a meeting next week with Bill McDade's brother Beach; he's brokering this deal with Wendt and the Aikens' and that could provide some answers. At least let me get a handle on this before you do anything Crafty-like."

"Sure, Louie, if I was ever to do something rash you would be the first to know, like always." They shared a laugh. "Small world, it's amazing how some of these dots connect when you consider your old friend's brother is directly in Wendt's sights. You know where to find me, here on the boat, at the Buc or in extreme cases maybe over at the Jetty. I'm not going to be roaming around much for the present. Keep me in mind, buddy."

"I'll call you on Tuesday. Behave yourself."

Crafty tossed the phone onto the L couch in the salon, got up out of his chair and went down to the head. 'Who is that guy looking back at you' the old mate asked the image in the mirror. 'Why does everything in this day and age have to be so damn complicated? His beard had busted out and his hair was down to his shoulders, a slight alteration made for concealment. He grabbed his hat and shades and took one last look at the guy in the mirror to see if he could recognize the man he was used to looking back at. 'It'll do for now even though that asshole Wendt will more than likely see right through it.'

He quickly ascended the steps up through the salon and slid open the double doors. Locking them behind him he placed the key in the bottom tackle drawer, and did a one two from the step to the covering board and finally the dock finger pier. Walking had become a major stress relief for the mate, and it was always an exercise with no plan or direction. The main benefit of his daily constitutional, as far as Crafty was concerned, was that it renewed his mind. It dimmed the bright glare of his present circumstances and moved him to start thinking about other things.

He wasn't at all a man accustomed to running from a situation. He had experienced the horrors of combat and although he had never been physically wounded, he succumbed to the same wrenching scars in the soul that he and all his brothers received. He worked through the pain with a little outside help from other vets, and with the understanding ear of the few close friends he had. Louis had always been there for him professionally of course, but the older captain had taken their relationship much further in ways that a father would love and discipline a son. He never took this for granted as his own father was not really that hands on, spending a good deal of time away from the home for various reasons.

Crafty could look back on his life and clearly see that he was a man usually eager for the fight, someone who had no problem facing inherent danger. He might even make the case he was addicted to the adrenalin as long as the danger was directly in front of him and he knew the source. This dark cloud hanging over him was a different specter of evil, without reason or any recognizable cue, save the one man alive he could connect to it. Crafty knew he and Louis had to expose Adam Wendt, and do it in a manner that would leave them blameless and finally set free from his control. But how?

Although he'd been walking for an hour, the mate suddenly grasped his surroundings and set his meditations aside for the moment. He was standing where the old Colonnades Hotel once stood adjacent Riviera Beach. In the early days this place had been the hangout for many celebrities and politicians; a nice place to beach it and drink, swap lies and get lucky perhaps. 'MacArthur had the right idea he thought,' at least until the 90's when the landmark was leveled to make way for more condos. 'That sucks, that really pisses me off more than anything in this day and age. People who have to live on the beach and don't interact with the water; and all those newer, faster, bigger fishing boats that jam the marinas rarely untying the lines. That I do not understand.'

Crafty suddenly heard the long blast of a train
horn nearly on top of him and cringed.

"Shit, Frankie, where did you get that thing?"

"Sounded like the East Coast railroad, didn't it; give you a start? Hop in we're going over to the Jetty to watch the game."

"I'magine. You are headed back to the boat eventually aren't you?"

"Yeah, fishing tomorrow, a few boats headed out on a corporate junket. Get in old man we'll keep an eye on 'ya."

"Might as well, Frankie, I'm just wandering around chasing my tail anyway."

The Jetty had way more than its fair share of stories of crews, fishermen and Singer Island over the years. Unfortunately, the mental capacity of the storyteller[s] whether influenced by booze or other substances, the time of day or just a sincere desire to entertain, often resulted in conflicting versions of these episodes down the line. But...that was the aura of the joint, where the endings almost always concluded with the old tag, 'you can't make this stuff up.'

When the three sailors walked in it was nearly nine, predictably too early an hour for things to get that interesting at the bar. Crafty felt the sticky floor grabbing his deck shoes with every step as they moved on to the bar proper and took a stool. Crafty had known Frankie for years and had a great deal of respect for the man, both for his fishing prowess and his refusal to weave stretch into his 'fish tales.'

The third man was a very young captain he had met last month at the marina, who had brought the boat down for an early winter stop, before continuing on down to the Yucatan in February. The 'kid' had a very nice ride in the form of a sixty two Spencer, but the general dock consensus was still in development, due to the fact that the vessel hadn't left the dock since its arrival. Crafty found the kid somewhat cocky in their first meeting, and had he been able to ID the shotgun rider in the dark, probably would not have jumped into the truck.

Three periods of hockey and five rounds of drinks later, the honkytonk had filled considerably with patrons, and the discussion amongst Crafty's crew had naturally turned to fishing.

"Heard about your run over in the Azores, Crafty, good going on that. Heard about the other bullshit too, is this thing ever going to quit dogging you?"

"Doesn't look like, Frankie, a lot of dark clouds following me around."

The kid looked up from his I-phone for the first time in

about thirty minutes, "What thing, dude? You get in a bind over there?"

"No." Crafty took a long pull on his Anejo and Coke as he briefly studied the kid, before staring back at the TV.

"Some of the locals there aren't totally happy about the increase in American crews thinning their charter pool," Frankie quickly chimed in realizing he might have spoken out of turn regarding his friend's predicament, "that's all."

"I Gotcha. Isla Mujeres is a pretty cool place from what I hear, don't expect to find much of that down there," sayeth the kid.

"You shouldn't if you're respectful of the folks and don't get a swelled head," Crafty responded.

"I treat people the way they treat me, but I work for the boss man. My job is to keep him happy and on fish as much as possible. When he's happy, the captain is happy," offered up the kid without looking up from the smart phone he was fingering to excess.

"That's the general idea, kid, putting it into practice sometimes calls for a little more creativity; like when you breakdown or one of the guests party's beyond the rules, or maybe your boss is so tight he simply squeezes the hair off a buffalo nickel. You're really the first line of defense for your owner, diplomacy does have its own rewards," spoke Capt. Frank to the newbie figuring he might provide some useful advice.

"Not that worried about it, Frankie, I can handle myself. I'll have a couple of guys in the pit taking care of baits and dredges, plus a man in the tower."

"That's all good, kid, but that ain't what I'm saying."

"I always steer clear of trouble, Frankie."

"Yeah…but if you don't plan for trouble, it will definitely come find you."

"Nah… we'll be alright."

Crafty was becoming increasingly more bored by the minute, and didn't much appreciate the arrogance of this obtuse young skipper. The old mate had by now cultivated a fair buzz, and he hadn't eaten a crumb since breakfast. He was getting stool sore and he began to feel the early twinges of potential whirlies when he spoke. "How many sails has your boss caught, anyway, kid?"

"A few, that's why he wanted to check Mexico out."

"Those fish can eat fast down there, kid, don't you think your boss would learn more without such a hidden presentation?"

"I don't follow you."

"The dredges, kid, I mean you're not fishing a tournament. How is he ever going to be a good hook dumping circle hooks all day live baiting dead bait?"

"That's what the guy in the tower is for."

"Look, kid, if you were fishing a tournament and the fleet had 'em all rounded up, you would be an idiot not to pull dredges. Your guy has caught only a handful of fish, however, and I think he would benefit from a more direct visual encounter on the surface. It's a lot more fun pulling a sail off a squid chain teaser than the guy upstairs yelling 'dump it' at the top of his lungs. He'll learn more about feel, fish movement and tendencies that way, the bite can be quite public down there."

"Not interested, the boss is all about the bottom line in everything under the sun. Flags on the 'riggers' is what he's looking for."

"You know kid...we never even flew flags down there, too much work at the end of the day. I'm sorry to hear that I really am, for you and your boss."

The kid looked up from his I-phone to take a break from his frenzied fingering of his little friend and stared back at Crafty for a moment. He wasn't sure what to say to the old mate, but he had to say something, "Dude, what exactly are you talking about?"

"What I'm talking about is going all that way to get a bunch of shots at sailfish, and then taking most of the fun and learning out of it by trying to out release everyone else. It's one thing when a seasoned crew agrees to make a statement and go all out for numbers, but you appear to be not quite ready for prime time on that score."

"What's that?" The kid is back on the smartphone once again.

"Kid… do you think you could put away your baby bottle for a little while, you might just learn something here."

"What the hell are you talking about old timer?"

"Pup, if that phone was a nipple it would never leave your mouth, that's what I'm talking about. I would be more than happy to stick it in there for you if you'd like."

Well, at this point in the 'discussion' the kid stood up, but stepped a little further away not quite sure what was coming next. In a split second Frankie jumped to his feet and stood between the two men and waved the kid to step away behind his back. "Crafty, what the hell is going on, this is exactly what you don't need right now! Let it rest, bro."

"Suppose so, Frankie. I'm walking back to the boat, see you tomorrow," the old mate slurred as he headed for the door.

"What's his problem, Frankie, dude's got attitude."

"Kid, that man has seen more sea buoys than you have telephone poles. You need to respect that or, in the very least, act like you have some respect. You got a lot to learn, boy; the man was only trying to show you a few short cuts. Look, he's been under a ton of stress lately, so just let it go at that," Frankie advised the young captain as the pair sat back down. Frankie, however, remained quite baffled and concerned over his friend's strange behavior.

* * * * * *

Bill McDade stepped out of his Ford 150 and walked to the chained gate at one of the ranch's many access points. Pulling a ring of keys from his hunting jacket, he began to sort through the dozen or so possibilities until he found the one stamped MDR for Melear Dairy Road, the small road they had just exited. Travelling almost a mile on the dirt road they had turned onto, led them to this pasture gate, the only break in the simple barbed wire fence that stretched for miles in either direction. The road ahead disappeared into a hammock for they were still a couple of miles from Beach McDade's office. Billy swung the hinged gate to the left in clearing the road, and then returned to his truck taking it through before getting out and locking the gate once more.

Louis had not been out here for many years, but was happy to see things had changed very little in his absence. Cows were still randomly distributed as far as the eye could see, grazing peacefully with the same white birds picking the insects off their backs. The going was slow as the washboard condition of the road indicated the need for some interval grading.

Passing through the first clump of trees, the road now opened to a fresh panorama of fields, cows and airborne turkey buzzards. A mile ahead, on a prominent rise, a beautiful oak forest provided a thick canopy for the hunting lodge and the utility barn which Beach McDade had adapted and climate controlled for the purposes of serving as his office. Louis was laughing to himself as Billy was idling through a small herd of turkeys not willing to clear the road in any kind of hurry.

"Guaranteed, Billy, if I had a gun, these birds would be

77

nowhere in sight."

"Naturally, Louis they're first cousins to crows! I, for one, am far more interested in what my brother has up his sleeve 'cause whenever that man gets this worked up over something like this deal, it's big. He's been quite reluctant to say anything over the land line; he's really some kind of paranoid regarding this play for the ranch. Can't wait to see what he throws at us."

"I just hope it gives us something to think about, a direction, a plan, something. Crafty, Cami and I are coming to the end of our rope, time to do something even if it's wrong. I don't think going to the authorities without a case is very wise either, there's no telling who might be on Wendt's payroll locally. With all this splash, he is bound to have at least one ear on the force. It's a tough call, and I just can't bring myself to make it."

The men parked in front of the open barn door and exited the truck. Once inside, Billy led Louis over to the walled off section of the structure in the far corner. The makeshift room had a door and two windows, one of plexiglas the other mostly taken up with the AC unit. The man inside motioned them in, but did not get up from his large drafting table.

"What's the good word, boys," Beach mumbled still pouring over large pages of white plans, surveys and other assorted documents. A tall cardboard box was stuffed full with rolled up 3x3 foot documents, and on the floor, similar rolls of paper lay strewn all over the place. The whole scene looked like something out of the reformation, as in the scholarly undertaking of translating the Dead Sea scrolls.

Beach continued to examine the material, going from one pile to the next, unrolling this chart only to roll it back up and exchange it for another, all the while humming some disjointed melody. He pretty much ignored his guests for the time being, until after about ten minutes he paused and looked up from the drafting table, "only be a minute, just want to be sure." In another ten minutes the longstanding foreman of the Aikens Ranch finally arose, and blessed the table and his findings with his two outstretched arms, "There it is, gentlemen."

"There what is my brother?"

"The kicker, Bill, the proverbial fly in the ointment so to speak."

"Well, Beachie, out with it! What do you got?"

The foreman began to pace around the office not paying much attention to all the white paper he was stepping on.

"Ok…….Adam Wendt by all accounts is poised and ready to follow through and submit a new contract on the ranch. After a few meetings with my guys, I know for certain they don't want to buy into a political problem down the line regarding the developmental rights attached to this property. They were on the fence for the most part, and these latest disclosures from Water Management have caused them to reconsider. In fact, they have already put a Contract on a large parcel near Thomasville, Georgia. They are not going to go hard on this deal, although they probably won't decline to go forward until the midnight hour as is the corporate custom."

"So you're saying Wendt now has clear sailing to get it."

"Yes, Bill, that is what I'm saying. His land planners have pretty much covered all the bases, and in some cases, have smartly just recertified a lot of the work done by my guys which is perfectly legal if undertaken within the time interval specified by law. Water issues, hydrology, traffic studies, species relocations you know gopher tortoises and kites, things like that which have already been reviewed; those issues can be signed off by the county and the state. Subsequent buyers need only recertify them within that certain time limit. Wendt is not going to begin to tackle site plan approval, DRI and land use change application with the state, until he has control of the property. Of that you can be sure. Wendt's team was very thorough environmentally as well. They did a huge phase one that would boggle the mind, hell, they did a phase two study of this entire pole barn, the lodge, and every equipment shack on the property. Clear sailing so far. Their many borings all over the ranch have given them a very good read of what they will need for their horizontal development in terms of fill, water and sewer, and possible income streams from any future mining permits that might be awarded the owners of the property. However, I would say that they weren't totally perfect."

"Looks like a lock for them, Beach," Louis conceded.

"Yes and no, Louie, look here," replied Beach as he returned to the drafting table waving the other two to look over his shoulder. "This is the preliminary site plan for the center, the footprint as it were," noted Beach as he circled the mechanically sketched dimensions of the various buildings comprising the first phase of construction." Very logical, I fully expected this would be the central location, based on my intimate knowledge of this place gained over the years. You probably didn't notice the slight rise of the land when you drove in, where we are standing right now." Beach chuckled a bit, "You know, boys, forty feet doesn't sound like much, but in terms of the south Florida flood plain it's practically a mountain. Look here."

Beach reached over to another chart and unrolled it laying it over the one already spread on the table. "This is a GIS topo map of the state, note the color coding of the various elevations here, and how it gives you very clear graphic illustration of height above sea level. You can easily see the 'spine' of Florida and the aquifer beneath it as it descends down primarily through the middle of the state from the north; the springs, the elevations around Lake City, down through Mt Dora etc., as it makes its way to a terminus just northwest of the lake, here. We are a hair northeast of the lake and due north of Port Mayaca, right here where the civil war Battle of Okeechobee was fought. If you take a good look at this topo you'll see that there is an offshoot to that spine here, pretty much where we are standing right now. It's not as spectacular as the elevations within the spine, but note that it is the highest elevation adjacent the big lake along its entire shoreline." With that declaration, Beach stepped back from the table with a smile and a nod of satisfaction.

"There's more, I hope," Bill McDade pressed his brother, "Beach?"

"Indeed, little brother, grab that box of cable flags over there, would you Billy. Here Louie hold on to this for a minute," instructed Beach as he passed Louis a hand held Garmin GPS. He then walked over to the adjacent wall and removed a T-shaped metal bar from its hanger, removing a tube that appeared threaded onto its downward base. What was left was a simple T of 3/8inch rebar, where the downward rod extended about four feet.

"Not fancy, but this should do the job, follow me on out, boys."

Beach led them to a small elevated clearing surrounded by majestic old oaks no more than a few hundred yards from the barn. He looked around at some of the larger trees and began to make orderly paces while traversing all across the clearing. "Let me have the Garmin will you, Louis." The foreman continued his pacing occasionally referring back to the GPS, then again to a sighting of a fixed landmark. This ritual went on for some time.

"Billy, if I tap the ground with the tip of my boot place one of those cable flags right there. Be careful not to disturb the ground, just poke the wire end in. We want to leave things as if they were unmolested if you know what I mean, just like you were marking a cable for the excavators."

"Done."

For the next hour, Beach McDade continued his pacing and reading of the GPS coordinates, along with referencing different landmarks at the same time, effectively creating a makeshift measurement of near Differential GPS accuracy. Wherever he tapped the soil with the tip of his boot, Billy would insert one of the cable flags into the ground. When he was satisfied that he had sufficiently 'mapped' the area, Beach gave the GPS back to Louis and took a final survey of the grounds. In total, his brother had placed about 100 of those cable flags into the soil. There was no observable order to the pattern that a submerged cable or gas line might have suggested, only a meandering line of flags displayed all across the clearing. Beach picked up the T-rod and made one last scan of the area.

"Looking for water now are we Beach," Billy teased looking over at Louis who had remained focused on the foreman's every move.

"Be patient little brother, I'm almost done," requested Beach as he made his first careful boring into the ground at the site of the first flag. He moved on to the next flag, making a similar boring at that location, and then another, and another until he had completed his borings guided by the entire grid of markers.

"I'm satisfied, things are still pretty much the same here," declared Beach as he sat down and lay against the trunk of a large oak. "Gentlemen, there is your fly in the ointment!"

"I think you need to expand on that big brother, you've been out in the sun too long."

The foreman began to laugh before measuring his thoughts, "All that due diligence they sent my way, the stacks of geological reports, the water issues, species relocations, Phase II environmental studies, upland/wetland delineations, so much of it redundant, so much of it recertified; information going this way studies going that way, it was an exhausting tour de force. In all that mess and confusion, however, there was one thing overlooked by both Buyers in their flawed due diligence. There was a kit that I never received. It rarely becomes an issue because statistically, it is usually a highly improbable situation. Nevertheless, the state and the applicant must sign off on it for site plan approval in declaring this project shovel ready.”

“And that would be, Beach,” Louis urged as he reset his Busch beer cap.

“Why… the archaeological study of course, Louis.”

“I see, you mean like arrowheads and Indian artifacts?”

“I think it’s something a little more significant than that, Louis. Gaze at all those markers for a second, and see if anything jumps out at you.”

Louis again removed his ball cap and scratched his head staring at all the flags. He walked around the clearing for a while, but had nothing to say.

Beach stood up and walked over to Louis and put his arm around his shoulder and began to draw a little figure with his pointer finger, “Okay, Louis, does this group here suggest any kind of shape to you?”

“Looks like a big chicken bone, a drumstick maybe.”

Laughter all around.

“Well…you’re getting warmer, but that would be a damn big bird wouldn’t it? You are right about one thing though, Louis, it is definitely a bone.” The implications of that last statement finally penetrated the thoughts of the foreman’s guests as they stared at one another in disbelief. “That’s right, boys, we’re talking about dinosaurs here. This figure right here was the only one Daddy uncovered, Billy, and he chipped off a piece and had it tested up in Gainesville. It's a hundred percent DNA certified dinosaur bone by the carbon dating, and this area we staked out today is only one of a few more. There're more bones over in that other hollow over there. Another one way out there, but I'm not exactly sure how many more there might be. Nothing like finding a whole skeleton quite yet, so far it would appear it's just a random assortment."

"What does this mean for Wendt," Billy queried his brother

"Well…here's the situation. This in and of itself won't kill the deal for Mr. Wendt over time, but I can tell you this, it will derail his timetable and put a huge hit on his wallet in new soft costs, and the extended challenges of carrying a project of this magnitude for an additional unknown period of time. He will not be pleased with this discovery, gentlemen, you have a real 'trip wire' here. I expect Wendt will have this property under contract by next week, and based on everything I've gone over, he and his gang will go hard on the deal within thirty days to the tune of twenty million dollars. We could let fly then or…wait until farther down the pipeline for DRI approval and Final Site Plan Approval, which would really chap his ass after spending all that additional capital with no developmental orders to show for it."

"I appreciate all this, Beach, but won't that delay whatever commission you're entitled to?"

"Louis, I'll get paid at the Closing by the Aikens once they have secured hard money as stated in the Contract. They will have a sizable deposit in hand with the balance coming in various releases concluding with Final Site Plan Approval; no other contingencies exist. Wendt could even run out of time on his CPUD and other entitlements granted from the county. The main thing is not to disturb anything, cross your fingers and hope that

Wendt goes hard on the deal without making this discovery."

"I see the light, brother. Louis and I will give this our undivided attention, as timing is going to be the key in all this."

"Think on it. Now you know why it was necessary for you to come out here. Stealth and more stealth, this knowledge doesn't go outside present company okay, our lives might depend on it," warned Beach as he began to carefully remove all the flags. "You'll know what I know when I know it."

"Thanks, Beach, for sharing this with us. I guess there's a whole lot more to this development game than one can learn from reading the paper."

"Happy to bring attention to it, Louis, I would have been ecstatic if my original guys had been able to take over the place for a few years. I could have disclosed everything that I have shown you in a timely manner and it would have worked its way through by the time they were ready to sell. They're sportsmen, cap, not developers. I just wanted to hang on to a bit of old Florida for a little while longer, before it's all gone."

"I gotcha real fine, Beach, no explanation necessary," Louis replied with a smile as hugged his old friend, "Let's hope with a little luck and some outside help we can redirect this threat into an early grave. I sure would like to see you stick around for a while out here." Louis shook the foreman's hand and started walking back to barn.

"All right big brother, Keep us in the loop as best you can. Louis and I will try to do the same from the waterfront. Be damn careful out here will you. Don't make yourself a headline." Billy hugged his brother one last time before making his way back to the truck.

$$* * * * * *$$

"Pretty work on your daily, Crafty, they were pretty scarce on that southwest wind yesterday."

"Thanks, Frankie, nice to be lucky. The Greek and his girlfriend caught everything we showed 'em, and the lady even prospected one up in the afternoon; pretty lucky to get five eaters up there." Crafty continued to prepare his 'corn cob' sized mullet for one of two double dredges he was going to pull in the morning. He had done the first prep months ago with the gutting and slimming of the fishes' profile with a football notch 'surgically' cut from the head; then a tubing out the backbone. From there the natural baits now ready for final rigging were immersed in overnight brine and then vacuumed sealed for the freezer, until now.

"All right, old timer, give me your take on yesterday."

"Come on, Capt. Frank, you've done this before. Light southwest, pre-front; you know the fish are more than likely going to get it done before noon. Then it's probably scatter and sulk until the real weather clocks around to compress them again."

"A lot of boats running all over the place, north and south, but I was around you all day, and there were just a few of us at the corner and we had it all to ourselves. Catch one from a double, and see another one caught; my sightings for the day. You and Emory see any more beside the five you caught?"

"Like I said… the four that we saw and the prospect. If you look back at the first day, it was a little stronger bite than yesterday, right there. A little more wind from the southeast, and a tad more current. The fish had better conditions then, but still, it didn't seem to stretch them out much."

"Meaning?"

"Frankie, as soon as the current flows north of Jupiter Inlet, I'm seeing it take a turn to the northeast at about thirty degrees. The Stuart boys were not seeing the fish, and most of them were finding the color change offshore the hill in 420 feet. Pretty deep water….and….talked to Louis last night and he told me everybody out of Ft. Pierce was running down to the 12A buoy to start fishing. The water temps have taken a nose dive up there, no bellies, no hook currents, no comfort stations. Bethel Shoal was in the 60's"

"Mark much bait?"

"Emory said he wasn't driving over any kind of bait he would usually like to fish on. I'll say this, Frankie; when they popped up they were working on flyers, sheets of 'em, all sizes. They were cutting through them, you know, on the surface, mostly 'rigger bites, a different look for a change, something out of the scrapbook."   Both men shared a laugh. Crafty offered up one more tidbit, "Last hour of the flood, and first hour of the ebb, by 1:00 it was over."

"Think this front is going to blow through like they're advertising? Kind of fair and balmy yesterday, boring westerly today."

"I do, Frankie, definitely. They're talking a dusting of snow in Jacksonville tomorrow, and the down current is screaming out of Stuart, green water temps dropping all afternoon yesterday." Crafty continued on as he laid the last of his mullet into the bait cooler. He then moved on to a second chest loaded to the brim with fresh caught ballyhoo in chip ice. "All right, Cap'n Frank, you have now picked my brains to the point of my pending mental exhaustion, and I've all these creatures to do," Crafty stated as he began loading the baitfish onto a hunting arrow to purge the ballyhoos' eye sockets of all membranes and eyeballs.

"Sorry, bud, I'll leave you alone," Frankie replied as he began to walk down the dock, "it's just that I value your opinion so much."

"Don't bust my balls and I won't yours," the mate yelled not looking up from his rigging.

"Can't… yours already been busted for a long time." They were good friends.

Crafty was quite happy to be fishing the tournament out of Sailfish Marina even though the boat was actually tied up at a private dock adjacent the north end of the public docks. The Gold Cup Team Tournament was not the oldest contest in big game fishing history, yet the Sailfish Club of Palm Beach is as historically relevant to Florida sail fishing, as Augusta is to Golf and the Masters. The beauty of it to Crafty was being the last entry allowed into the affair, and that the club marina did not have the space to provide the Greek's boat with a slip. 'Ideal' the mate thought to himself when Emory gave him the news, they would not have to make that dreaded round trip every day to the north end of the island to the club. You could leave the dock on fishing days whenever you chose, but the logistics of everything else was made far more convenient by staying on the north side of Lake Worth Inlet.

They had been lucky to catch five sails the day before, and with that daily in their pocket they had moved to third overall with half the tournament completed. The old mate had fished more tournaments than he could remember good or bad, and the prep rituals he was currently engaged in, were not that unique in any way. From salts to sea school grads, Crafty's way of doing and rigging things was emblematic of the art required in his chosen profession; all others vying for the prize had either attained matching skills, or were in the process of learning same.

Living on the boat this winter had given the old mate more time for retrospection, and in a providential sense, less time for distractions. Fishing and fishing tournaments had taken somewhat divergent paths for Crafty over the years, not just in tackle and techniques, but in old fashioned terms like fun and comradery. The mate had been an integral part in the evolution of sport fishing and his contributions had certainly left their mark with his peers. Crafty, however, would be the first to tell you that it was nearly impossible to keep that competitive edge with each passing year. Technology had created many pluses for the recreational fisherman, while at the same time marginalizing the lessons that years on the water might have instilled.

His attitude had changed. 'Better to be Lucky than Good', was an old adage that all fishermen could, and in most cases do stand behind. Crafty was always charitable in publicly relating that sentiment in every fish story he ever told, though in secret, he regarded the act of fishing as a virtual conversation with nature. A day fishing a tourney was no different than a day's fishing, period. He would fish just as hard every day he untied the lines, regardless of the up tick at the end of the day. In these times of sunset retrospection, he knew perfectly well the accounting of his treasured memories, and they rarely involved tournaments. One Captain, one mate, and more than likely, one to four anglers that ran the gamut from tyro to ringer; could not be expected to hold up over time against a bigger, much faster boat with a crew of seven, four ringers and the financial ability to outspend the competition. 'No disputing that fact,' Crafty considered, no disputing the ever shrinking field of participants as well. What had old man Evinrude lectured him on at three in the morning in San Salvador over a near empty bottle of Jack Daniels…"Crafty, my good man, you can work with progress to your advantage, but I'll guarantee you'll fade away trying to stop it."

The old businessman was certainly right about that. Going with your gut is a decidedly different act for the fisherman than doing all the right things and waiting for the bottom line. But he was Crafty, and he was going to construct a trolling spread to entice the creatures to the best of his ability, with whatever tools and resources he was given. Perhaps now, this sentiment would especially apply to the two legged creatures as well. Crafty was always appreciative in noting the providential timing of his arrival in this fishing game. Looking back, 'we caught a lot more with a lot less'. He had seen and experienced awesome displays of nature in ways that might never be seen again. 'Timing is everything,' he concluded, 'whether by my hand or another, it has always been good to me.'

"How we doing, need a hand with anything,Crafty," Emory asked from the dock as he approached the transom of the Brother's Pride.

"I think we're looking good, Emory. Dredged up with mullet and ballyhoo, and a cooler full of bullets; stripped some line off, and retied doubles and all. The rest of it can wait until morning."

"Cool. Supposed to blow like stink out of the west northwest tomorrow, should be interesting, got any ideas ol'boy?"

"You mean like running up to the 500 line?" Both men shared a laugh.

"Yeah…well… we're just close enough to the top to not get off our game plan for the moment, planning on going right back there. Besides, the ocean is going to be a lot nicer down at this end under the beach."

"Absolutely, Emory, got my vote. The Greek has never been one to take the fun out of it anyway, and he's hot on this gal and she loves to fish. Why would he want to put such a beautiful combination to the test?"

"Roger that. I guess we'll pull out of here around seven thirty or so, or whenever they stroll down from the house. Just got to run a few miles to the north under the beach, maybe leave late with some stealth."

"It's the right move, Emory, those fish that have been here could be off Ocean Reef by now, but I doubt it. What's coming from the north is anybody's guess looking at the inshore water temps dropping so fast. If they're tailing along with that white spot on their head, they have a better chance of waking up when they hit the warmer water, if that change is still there in the morning."

"Exactly, I agree. All right, Crafty got to fly. The boss wants me to go to the dog track with them as designated driver. The gloves can't make it tonight, he's down in Lauderdale having dinner with his sister. You're sure you don't need a hand with anything?"

"Nah…got it covered, Emory, we're good. See you in the am for coffee."

"Yes sir. Hey….Timmy over on the charter dock fished today; go see if you can get some intel."

"Did…two on live bait, a couple decent mahis, but Timmy said they were fussy as shit. He did all his business before noon."

"Gotcha fine. Seeya."

By default, Emory was the last boat to untie the lines the following morning, charter boats included. When the Greek and his girl finally made their way down from the house it was ten to eight. It had been a night of too much fun that ended up at a gentleman's club somewhere west of the airport. The Greek's intentions were aimed more at the aged prime steaks and wine cellar the joint was famous for rather than the entertainment.

The Greek had hit a tri-box to the tune of $1800, and 'found' money always burned through his pockets.

In five minutes the Brother's Pride was up on plane running north, not far outside the surf break in front of condo row on Singer Island. It was blowing hard from the northwest, but the seas in the lee under the beach were only a 2 foot chop. Dillon switched the radar to transmit and painted a number of targets stretching from Boynton Inlet on up to nearly the St Lucie Inlet off Stuart. His tactical guess of the early morning called for a significant color change in around 180-200 feet of water as had been the case in preceding fishing days. Looking at the targets and their alignment to the north would tend to substantiate his reasoning. He was cruising along in 27 feet of water, however, and would not make that easterly tack until almost at like latitude with his own informal waypoint.

Emory left the helm chair with the boat on autopilot and looked down into the pit, noting the two double dredges that Crafty had ready and baited up, mullet on the left side ballyhoo on the right. Crafty was going over his rods, line, hooks and knots in the crowded rocket launcher a final time.

"Damn water is cold as shit," Capt. Emory spoke out loud to himself, "even looks cold." The Garmin said 68 degreesF, 'probably right on, got no reason to doubt it.' The sea had become a very opaque blended green, a change from the shiny aquamarine of recent days. In wind conditions like these the offshore horizon usually provided a clear profile of large swells, created by unprotected wind swept seas kicked up even higher by the opposing northerly currents of the Gulf Stream. That did not seem to be the case today; it was a frigid January morning of bluebird skies and half dozen layers of clothing were barely keeping the captain comfortable.

At eight fifteen Emory made his right turn until he was in 150 feet of water. He powered down the boat to idle speed and began to unleash the safety lines of his outriggers. In a manner of seconds they were deployed away from the boat, as Crafty adjusted halyard tension from the cockpit. The dredges were connected to a pulley system managed by Emory's electric reels from above, and then last, all four fishing lines were baited.

"Lines in three minutes," Dillon called out to the team.

Crafty completed his setup by shitting and performing the needed chiropractic on his four ballyhoo, while the Greek and his gal adjusted their respective gimbal belts. The team was ready and all was quiet as Capt. Dillon put the vessel in a down sea tack.

"Put 'em in!"

Everyone went to work in a smooth unhurried pace. The two anglers each let out flat line bait a specified distance behind the boat, just beyond a point where the submerged dredges would be set. The pair set their rods into the rod holder at each corner where the transom joined the side of the hull, making sure there was no drag, and activated the clickers in the reel. The Greek looked over at his partner while he pulled a few feet of line off the reel, made a series of five or so twists to create a loop which he then fastened to a release clip mounted on the rub rail directly below the rod tip. This setup on the flat lines would provide immediate drop back to a quick sail bite with a drag free set up giving the angler time to get to the rod.

Crafty had deployed both outrigger baits to a distance a little more than twice that of the inside baits, making a final adjustment of rigger extension height and distance where experience told him the baits were working at their best. This fairly standard bait spread utilizing dredge teasers usually saw a majority of first encounters to the inside baits, and in practice, this is where the majority of initial hookups would come. Outrigger baits come more into play when other fish enter the spread after initial activity, when the boat is turned into a hooked fish, or times when conditions are so calm the predators are just lazy and fade off the inside part of the spread. This thinking, of course, is a major oversimplification; but when conditions are good and there is a good supply of sails in the area, most bites will come to the area of flat lines and the dredges below.

Crafty had the right ballyhoo dredge already in the water, and was now lifting the heavier mullet dredge over the side, the lead dredge and lead in left hand the secondary dredge in the right. At once the mate noted he had a spinner on the rear dredge and put the whole mess back in the boat. He undid the condemned fish and could see that its head had a hard to see crack, before tossing it into a bucket. He clipped a fresh fish back into the dredge, and started again by dropping the rear and then the lead dredge and lead weight into the water in a fluid motion. Taking a wrap of teaser line he held the full teaser near the boat where it could be viewed submerged one final time. It was working flawlessly with each member of the grouping swimming in sync; a fresh natural ball of swimming baits, it was the hands down choice of teasers for 99.9% of all sailfish tournament teams.

Emory had been observing Crafty's activity from the bridge throughout the test run, "Looking good from here, man, ready when you are." The captain hollered down as he prepared to back the drag off the electric reel from above. The mate then released his rigged temptation as Emory let the teaser run out and deeper away from the boat. The captain did not get to view his teaser for very long, as just a few feet under the clear view of the teaser all but disappeared into the unusually opaque water. He stopped the bridge reel and positioned the dredge at a distance more indicated by where the line entered the water. For the only time he could actually see the dredge from the bridge, was with some helpful backlighting and sun, and even at these times it was indistinct with only a subtle outline. Emory had fished in every type of ocean imaginable, from gem quality indigo to army green and even on to hideous bodies of brown and dark water. He had good eyes, but he could not recall seeing any water more impenetrable than he was seeing today. He'd caught many sails in dirty brown conditions, but even those conditions seemed less muddied than today's ocean surface. It was not dirty, it was what the guys would probably classify as an okay green, but it was as opaque a body of water that he could ever remember. He straightened the boat out and examined the entrance points of his two dredges, and decided that they were a proper distance from the boat, albeit not very distinguishable. 'Screw it, I'm leaving them there.'

An hour had passed and the team on Brother's pride had but one 'public' bite of a kingfish that had sky rocketed fifteen feet out of the sea and cut an outrigger bait. In his group east of Jupiter inlet he counted ten other boats, and there had been one sailfish released. It was the sole release of the morning by Gold Cup boats. Emory was not dismayed however, as the incoming tide was just now starting to energize, and central to his day's plan was bite timing with the flood tide. The offshore side of the change he and his competitors were fishing was a dull blue; the inshore side was the very green water he'd been scratching his head over. It was here where he had gotten all the sail bites during the first two days of fishing, enough bites to have him in third at this point. If his theorizing was correct, the flying fish should be making a showing any time now.

The color sounder remained unchanged from two days ago;

some bottom markings, a few targets draped in mid-level ocean depth, probably kings, but no real good marks that would indicate the kind of bait sailfish would be working on. 'It'll happen here, if it happens anywhere,' the captain thought to himself. 'Got to'. Right now he was the only one fishing in the colder green water now showing a 72 degree temperature.

"Big sheets of flyers getting up over there Emory, 'bout a hundred yards off the port," Crafty alerted from the cockpit.

The captain followed his mate's arm to the point in the sea where hundreds of flying fish were exiting the water. Another wave hit the air, and underneath a big bull dolphin showed plenty of head as he pushed a lot of water with his high brow in his stalking. With each passing minute this scenario was repeating itself with greater numbers of flying fish continually breaking the surface.

Emory put the boat into a hard port turn into latest area of flyers he had seen, whipping the opposite outrigger bait into a skipping frenzy barely in the water. In an instant there he was, black as the ace of spades, in stark contrast against the powdery green water. If it hadn't been for the prominent extended dorsal fin he'd probably never identified him. "Left rigger… that was him, Crafty!"

The Greek got to the rod and set up in free spool putting the butt in his fishing belt. There was no feel right away, perhaps the fish was charging him or maybe he countered back to take another bait. Either way, he began his sensitivity training on closing the distance between he and fish, going into the slightest of drag on the circle hook he believed to be with the fish. As the man slowly went up on the drag lever, a loop in the line came visible. "He's got it!"

The Greek let the increasing drag do its work on bringing the hook from somewhere deep in the fish back towards its mouth, [or maybe it was already there] where it would find a solid and statistically desirable hook placement. This by all accounts and research is what circle hooks do. The ever increasing rod bend now confirmed that the sailfish indeed was hooked for the time being.

Emory turned slowly into the fish and scanned the rest of the spread to find nothing else in the baits. Retrieving his dredges to pre-selected 'stops' on the electric reels he called down to Crafty, "Let's go get him, they're pretty scarce this morning, man."

"Indeed, cap," the mate hollered back up as he cranked the other rigger bait to the pin and cleared both flat lines.

The sailfish burst into view a hundred feet from the back of the boat, gyrating into a sustained window wiping shaking of his head. The creature was pretty lit up now as his second exit from the water had him tail walking away from the boat for nearly fifty yards. He did settle down a might after that opening act, and began a slow descent pulling some drag.

Emory initiated a moderate backing down in reverse to close in on the fishes' position keeping the entry point of the fishing line as close to dead astern as possible. The next time the fish came into view he was only fifty to sixty feet off the back of the boat, and his coloration had dulled significantly. "Let's try him," Emory alerted as he began a more aggressive backing to the fish. When the fish was cruising off the right corner of the cockpit looking back, Dillon dug the starboard engine hard in reverse, and presented the leader to his mate's outstretched left arm. From there it was a simple wrap and a knife to the leader. Dillon called in the release to Buccaneer Bob.

The teasers and bait spread were quickly reset by the crew, and the Brothers Pride was back at it tacking toward and carving figure eights wherever the showers of flying fish busted the surface, only occasionally making a tack through the color change itself. Emory had chosen to commit to fishing the green water almost exclusively if for no other reason than he had not gotten one sail bite on the bluer side. There they had been jumped by a decent dolphin of 20 plus pounds, but Crafty quickly cut the fish off and replaced the rod with a ready backup.

Capt. Emory had done his best to understate his aggressive backing in the final play on his first fish, but turbo lag had caused his starboard engine to blow a good deal of smoke in that last dig at the fish. Now, he was looking at mostly bows of the nearby fleet, he knew that he had been made. In minutes, there would be a lot more boats fishing the green water inside the change. 'Bring it on' he thought to himself, 'there's a lot happening on the surface right now, just got to stay one fish ahead of the game.'

By eleven the wind had freshened to about 20 knots, but the bait showers did not let up one bit. Bonita boils and dolphin freight training on the surface added to the mix of predators cutting through and exploding on the constantly busting waves of flyers. Dillon was quite thankful for his luck in avoiding the Bonita, but he needed another fish as a few more sail releases were radioed in from a few of the fleet that had recently joined him on the green side. Coupled with the fact that this area was the only one producing sail, it would soon see an invasion of many more boats. A quick northerly scan to the horizon already painted four boats running at him at speed made easy in the down sea tack.

Another great flurry and then shower after shower of small flyers broke outside his right outrigger. Emory made a counter turn to starboard and whipped the right rigger in much the same fashion as he did with the first sail. A more aggressive bite, the sailfish cut the surface and crashed the bait showing a good deal more dorsal this time. The fish had committed suicide, screaming line away from the boat, and the Greeks girlfriend had shown very good speed in getting to the rod in time for the setup. With ease she had found fish, and that sail was grey hounding away from the boat. They were still in the hard turn to starboard, but by now Capt. Emory had focused his eyes on the opposite outrigger knowing that the bait was now sinking and slowing down as a result of the boat's turning into it. He could see the line tension coming and going, until seconds later the rigger clip bowed down and held some tension but not enough to pull the line from the clip.

"Left rigger, Tony, might have to try him through the clip!"

"On it," the Greek shouted back, he knew the drill. Quickly grabbing the rod from the rocket launcher he got set up in the belt and pointed the rod tip directly at the outrigger clip, his thumb caressing the spool. Without any help or pressure from the angler, the slight tugging on the clip bowed down a hair more, and the Greek decided to feed the fish through the clip itself, "I got you now, thin lips." Whether the line was released or not, from here the idea was the same, bring the drag up and take a peek so to speak. There was nothing under his thumb to indicate any fish movement down there, but he closed the reel and began to apply drag pressure. Nada, no feel and he was now at the preset button, 'fish is coming at me, dammit.' He started to crank out the bow in the slack line and in a manner of seconds, the line ripped from the rigger clip, the angler got the first feel of a rod bend, and sailfish was on his tail making a mess just about under the left rigger.

"Chrissy, back your drag off carefully and let that fish go on out, away from the boat. We're going to try Tony's fish first," Dillon hollered from above. It was the right move as her fish had settled down a hundred yards off the right rigger, and now Emory could pull off slightly and work on the smaller fish Tony had on. Their good luck continued to build with the second bite from the five foot juvenile sail, and once settled down he came right in never getting social or crossed up with the other larger fish still a good distance off the boat. Soon, they let the peewee go and continued a deliberate backing toward the second fish until the boat was nearly on top of the line where it entered the sea.

Crafty gave a hold up signal to the bridge when the fish started to sound. "This one's a pretty good swimmer, Emory; let him pull some drag for a minute. When the line ceased to pull off the reel, Chrissy went back up to the button and began her pumps to lift the fish. She was good, she knew how to get maximum benefit from the rod, and in five minutes the big sail was cruising from left to right 50 feet behind the boat.

"I'm going to use quick short pumps, I'll walk back from the transom when I think you can reach him Crafty," she yelled over the wind and engines.

"Sounds like a plan."

In another minute the outstretched arm of the old mate had a hank of leader in his right hand as he watched a sudden burst from the big sail pop the 60 pound. "We got him, reported the mate showing a ball of 60 pound leader up to the Cap.

"Buccaneer, Bob…boat forty, one for Tony, one for Chris right now."

"Take 117 and 118," came the reply from the VHF.

"Thank you, Bob." Three for three on another slow day. 'Lucky boy you are,' Emory thought to himself.

A few of the boats that joined him early on had released some sail; in fact one boat caught a triple and moved ahead on time for the daily. No matter, the team had held their position which turned out to be a very good thing as nearly all the tournament boats had by now invaded the area, bringing the flowers with them.

And just like that the bite was over; nature had shut off the switch. The flying fish and the birds disappeared, and save a few slicks leftover from the morning's feeding, all surface activity ceased. Game over.

The fleet continued to work hard on the fish, carving their turns and figure eights, but to no avail. Some went back to the blue water, some wandered out to three or four hundred feet and back into the shallows. It seemed everyone was committed to waiting them out for a late bite. When three o'clock rolled around, forty sport fishing boats crowded together and pounded the area of the morning's limited action. There was no afternoon bite, no flying fish and nothing but crying towels on the radio.

When Brother's Pride pulled into her slip behind the Greek's house they were still in third place, two fish behind the leader, second place boat had them on time. The wind was still howling out of the west northwest, and it was pretty damn cold by Palm Beach standards when the sun went down. The boat was caked with salt, and even by spreader lights it would be hard to give her a good cleaning.

"Nice going today, guys, tough fishing today, but you dealt us a few," the Greek spoke as he stepped onto the dock preparing to lift his honey up to the finger pier. Man, it's in the forties already and you got a lot to do. Give her a good rinse and we'll pretty her up when this thing is over tomorrow. Gloves will be back by then to help."

"Sounds good boss, we'll take good care of her," Emory replied as he closed up his electronics. See you guys in the morning."

Everyone who has spent a life at sea has their own stories of danger. It might involve a sinking, a big badass fish on the leader taking someone overboard or in rare occasions jumping into the boat, or maybe just a hook buried in the flesh of a poor fisherman. There have been more than a few captains that have been the victims of electrocution; there is no small number of very experienced men who slipped or stepped wrong coming down from the tower. It's part of the mix, you'll have that. More often than not, it's the habitual that is taken for granted, that motion you have done so many times suddenly trips you up with painful consequences.

Maybe it was the fading light of day or the slick surface of a heavy salt build up. It could have been the fact the step box was emptied of its contents prior to being placed in the cockpit sole. Or could it have been the fact the hinges were facing away from the person getting ready to board; or maybe just a combination of all of the above. But when Capt. Emory leaped from the covering board to the step box on the floor of the cockpit, something he might have executed thousands of times successfully, the last thing he expected was the lid to fly up and the box to skid four feet. He was instantly adrenalized when everything from the waist down gave way. He could have severely hit his head on the covering board, but dodged at least one bullet by instinctively grabbing the stainless banjo holder supporting the shore cord in the rod holder.

Lucky in that there was no blood or fractures, but unlucky as the captain heard the telltale sounds of tearing tissue just before the burn and searing pain in his right shoulder. "Shit! Oh man," Dillon moaned. "Crafty, where are y'at?"

* * * * * *

Louis threw another log on the fire to warm the cabin from the effects of low forty temperatures and the gusty winds howling outside. He reset the screen around the fireplace and went to finish what was left of the coffee when he heard his cell phone go off. It was about eight o'clock.

"Hey Crafty, what's going on, you still in the hunt?"

"Did ok for today, Louis, saw three caught three. We're still in third, Frankie has got us on time, and Jimmy's leading the thing by catching a triple this morning."

"I got you, glad to hear that. Don't sound like the count was too good today."

"Less than a fish per boat, only twenty seven according to Bob."

"How about some particulars."

"Fishing in funky chilly green water of 71.5, the only real bait around are stacks of flyers showering everywhere when it's going off. We started the day with the right guess at the corner on a blended milky green to dull blue color change, mainly on the consistency of the first two days keeping us near the top."

"Not a lot of current pushing through there sounds like."

"That's right, not a well-defined edge at all, no grass to speak of, if I saw any it was brown and dying."

"Hmmm…not so good, current and warm water could be a ways off."

"We've pretty much had the same pattern going all three days, although it has died somewhat with each passing day. Tuesday, they bit hard on the first hour of the flood, did a little in the afternoon on the break of the tide. Same thing Wednesday, good morning bite clocked ahead forty five minutes or so, then a quick flurry at the afternoon break. Today, it seems like everything kind of folded over with the bite backing up an hour, and they shut their mouths for the rest of the day. Dead.”

“I find it interesting that they were working on the flying fish that hard; haven’t seen that kind of activity much in recent years. If conditions ever get right on the edge it sounds like the bite could really pick up some.”

“Louis, you and I have fished around enough in this world to the point where we’ve been faced with nearly all possible water issues, wouldn’t you say?”

“That’s a fair statement.”

“Well…this water I have been fishing in, you know cold and green, takes the term powdery to a new level, totally unlike the powder blue stuff we see in the keys once in a while.”

“Kicked up is it. Big swell?”

“Not really, cap, looking offshore all day I never saw those big swells pushing and shoving down the beach; some three to four foot ‘peelers’ breaking on the beach maybe. It’s all about the water we’re fishing in, you just can’t see too far into the stuff, different.”

“I remember seeing those conditions in ’77 when the big freeze took out all the Australian Pines. That was a crazy day in February, so much sea smoke on push button hill, I couldn’t see the tips of my outriggers. It snowed in Stuart that morning.”

“Another mystery.”

“Be glad for the flying fish, I guess. You know… the unseasonably cold water has probably stunned them a little as well. Could be that an advantage has tipped the scale in favor of the sails.”

“You might be right, never considered that. Well, Louis, I

appreciate the input, but here is why I'm calling you at eight in the evening."

"Yes, Crafty."

"Emory took a tumble in the cockpit late this afternoon, but was able to break his fall by grabbing the banjo holder on the way down. Unfortunately, he torqued his right shoulder bad and the MRI shows a bad tear in the rotator cuff. Just found out, that's where we're at now at St. Mary's. He's all wrapped up in a sling, not to mention the medications; they're going to cut him next week. There's no way he's going to be able to drive that boat tomorrow."

"Sounds like…you find someone yet?"

"I have now, Captain Louie."

"You think that's wise? You know Wendt's fishing with Flores don't you."

"I do…but we're not tied up at the club, we're still behind the Greek's house. They couldn't fit us in over there. We get on the radio at seven sharp and sneak in a quick, low key substitution and you're in. I hadn't figured you to make the awards dinner, however." A brief laugh was shared.

"You run this by Emory? I don't want to make waves."

"Louis, it was his idea to call you first. He'd like to win this thing for the Greek and his new girl. You'll like her for all the right reasons."

"All right, Crafty… I'll see what I can do. What time at the boat?"

"Six for coffee, Emory will ride up top with you."

"Six then… I better get off this thing I have some prep to do before the morning."

"Thanks 'ol boy, finest kind."

"Seeya."

The prospect of going back to sea had Louis up at four thirty, energized and happy to be fishing again. He didn't want to wake his bride, so he quietly eased out of bed and went into the kitchen to start the coffee. He stared at the many layers of clothing he had set out the night before on the kitchen table and was satisfied they would be adequate; t shirt, long sleeve t shirt, skivvies, sweatshirt, jeans, sweat pants, and blue windbreaker. He was shivering looking at the dead fire and he went right to work in getting dressed.

He had prepared for the day making some terminal tackle the night before and he had put it all in a plastic bag right next to his fishing glasses on the kitchen table. He filled his 'to go' cup with coffee to the brim, grabbed his shades and made his way to the door. He tried his best to be quiet exiting the cabin when he heard her soft voice, "Good luck, old dog." He whispered a thank you and softly closed the squeaky door.

Walking up the hill and passing by McDade's house on the dirt drive that led out to the graveled street, he noticed the wind had let up some, and that it had backed up to more of a westerly now than northwest. 'Perhaps this trend might continue' he thought, 'maybe the high pressure is coming to us, can't hurt, wind might clock around…we'll see.' Louis made a left on the dead end dirt road that serviced the few houses that were north of the county line. In about a hundred yards the makeshift driveway terminated in a roughly carved turnaround where he always parked the old 150 while staying at the cabin.

Louis had decided to take the old way down to Singer

Island, through Hobe Sound on A1A, US 1 on into Jupiter, back to A1A down thru Juno where he might catch a good view of the ocean at first light, and then finally back on US 1 to Blue Heron in Riviera Beach and over to the boat.

He parked in the north corner of Sailfish Marina, grabbed his gear and hoofed it over to the dock next door. As he approached the Brother's Pride, he could see Emory and Crafty around the coffee table in the lighted salon. He carefully boarded the boat via covering board and step box, and by the time he reached the salon double doors they flew open.

"Hola, Cuban Louie," Emory rose and put his good arm around his old friend, "thanks for doing this, as you can see I really did myself this time."

"Don't feel too bad, Emory, I actually walked right off a dock once. After years being in the same slip, someone had actually moved the boat over to another slip three over. Wasn't paying much attention in those days and I walked right into a hole."

"Who moved the boat on you?"

"Why me, of course, the day before!"

Laughter all around.

"I'm assuming Crafty brought you up to date on where we sit. We've been hugging the corner for three days and have been lucky to catch eleven in what I'm sure the three of us would call slow fishing. It has all been about the flyers, they're showering everywhere when the bite is on. There's some decent Mahi and boneheads in the mix as well, although we have been extremely fortunate not to have driven over too many of them. Having said that, Louis, the afternoon bite has been diminishing with each passing day until yesterday, it was non-existent."

"Crafty said you guys were getting all your bites in the green side of the change, in some weird powdery water. That right?

"Yeah…really strange…very opaque stuff."

"Kind of like the back side of Gun Cay when it's blowing like stink."

"A little more to the green but the same look."

"I can only tell you that I've seen that condition once before, during the hard freeze of '77. You remember, Crafty, I know you were just starting out in Palm Beach with Jackie. Valentine's Day, 1977… the sails were on the surface balling the bait all afternoon; as far as you could see there were dorsals cutting."

"I remember, Louis, we ran out of live bait, ran out of frozen sardines, and just fished until they had literally eaten us up. We caught thirty seven that day backing and pitching baits, some boats did even better. Never seen it like that since."

"Nor I, but a few weeks before that day I remember seeing conditions like you have been fishing, and I tried a few things that definitely brought me a surplus of bites. Well… I'm the last man in, however, and Emory will be up top. I'm just a designated pair of hands on the wheel; this is the last day and you guys need to stick to your game plan."

"Thanks for the nod, Louis, appreciate that, but you have a whole lot more time on me fishing these Florida waters and if you have something to suggest come out with it," prodded the injured captain.

"Alright…the way I see it, these fish do have a little edge working on these flyers in such extreme conditions. The bait probably has been stunned a little from the cold water and the sails are taking advantage of it, it's the only game in town and they're probably getting ready to book south anyway."

"What would you do different, Louis, presentation, speed, got anything up your sleeve," Crafty queried as he got up to make another pot of coffee.

"What are you pulling for dredges?"

"Mullet and ballyhoo each on a side all naked."

"OK… leave the mullet dredge in place where you have been fishing it, but ditch the ballyhoo dredge. Instead, I want you to make a daisy chain of natural ballyhoo, and slide one of these down each of the individual baits in the chain." Louis emptied his bag on the table and a dozen blue and white sea witches fell out."

"Nice, Louis, tie those last night?" Emory picked up one for inspection, "I like the trim and salt and pepper concept, they shine nice too when you hold one up to the light. Pretty."

"Went to work after Crafty called me, had a bunch of that old hair, you know the Du Pont Mylar white you can't seem to find anymore, and I mixed them up with various amounts of that royal blue which also shines well. You know what the bass pros do after a lot of rain, go bright and go day glo." Laughter. "Pull your natural blue and white bally chain behind just enough trolling lead to keep the nose in the water, probably four to six ounces. Then…pull it a short rigger distance off the boat, so we can whip it in turns without any crossing problems. The rest of these slide down on your outrigger baits, oh, and the side you pull the daisy chain set a short rigger behind it."

"No flat line?"

"Not on that side. What you boys have described leads me to believe that the dredges have been somewhat neutralized by these conditions; at least as far as their effectiveness in the water column where the bite is taking place. Emory, are you marking anything that might paint a thermocline on the sounder?"

"You know, Louie, I have…yes. Yesterday it was a lot deeper than in previous days."

"Hmmm…well… keep the mullet dredge in the water, it may prove handy in turns as it drops. Okay, boys, you asked me, this is what I might do taking everything into consideration that you have told me. What about up top, the controls, anything I should know, Emory?"

"Typical pod, Louis, Mathers electronic, slow and fast idle, window synchronizing. I got trolling valves which I don't bother with when trolling," laughter around, "Just use them when I'm live baiting."

"Great. If you guys want to try some of this, cool. If not, also very cool. Like I said, I'm the last man in."

"Nice speech, Louis," Emory noted as he rose, "But as senior captain on this rig, I say we present a la 'Cuban Louie.' If it doesn't pan out we'll go back to plan A. All agreed on that?"

The three men nodded silently as they stood and placed their hands together in a three way grip.

Earlier on that Saturday morning, a groggy and sleep deprived Adam Wendt stared at the Keurig waiting for his double load of Kona to fill his mug. He then took a pull on the eye-opener with as much abandon as the hot temperatures would allow as he returned to the master bedroom to finish getting dressed for the final day of the Gold Cup.

"Ladies, just let yourselves out whenever, and lock the door behind you. My housekeeper has her own key and will be along this afternoon. I've left something for each of you on the island counter in the kitchen; thank you both for a very enjoyable evening. We should do this again in the not too distant future." Wendt made a final inspection of his world famous visage before grabbing a pair of cell phones as he headed out.

Wendt elected to head south on Broadway before turning off at sixth street heading to the west side of Lake Worth. The LCD on the dash of his Porsche lit up with the audio cue of an incoming call. He quickly previewed the caller ID and was immediately stoked at the timing of such a call, "Must be something for you to be calling me at this hour."

"Isn't this why you have me sitting here picking my feet day in and day out?"

"Get to the point, I'm on my way to the Sailfish Club to wrap up this fishing tournament."

"There's a new guy up on the bridge of the target boat I haven't seen before, and it looked as though he was checking everything out up there. The same captain is also up there, but he was just standing around while this new dude was familiarizing himself with the layout. When it pulled away from the dock, the new guy was at the helm."

"Really...young guy, old guy what?"

"An older dude, but everyone on the boat acted like they knew him. I've never seen him before this morning. Oh and the regular captain, he's all wrapped up in some kind of sling or something"

"Ok...good work, I'm glad you called. I want you to wait for the boat to come in and stay on whoever that was that jumped on this morning. Be ready to follow him and see where he leads you; and I mean stay on him till you find out where he's living or who he's screwing. Do your job."

"Count on it."

"I am...bring me something and I will be most appreciative as always."

Emory had the engines running when the Greek and his girlfriend jumped on the boat at around seven thirty. Louis stood at the helm while Dillon set up and initialized all the electronics.

"Hello, Louis, long time no see," the Greek yelled up to the bridge as he helped the pretty young lady onto the boat. "Glad to have you with us, my crew made a point of having you join us as a result of my captain's bad luck. I appreciate his honesty in stating he was not fit to run the boat. We are lucky to have such an experienced man at such short notice."

"Believe me, Tony, the pleasure is all mine. I hope I can add to the team, y'all have done quite well given the circumstances and the conditions."

"We have been lucky, Louie, and my Chrissy has been steady for us. Thanks again for filling in."

In five minutes Louis had the boat running north under the beach, repeating the boat's track yesterday as recorded on the plotter. The wind had backed a little during the night and had dropped to a more moderate 12 to 15 knots. Louis scanned the eastern horizon and saw nothing to indicate the presence of any northerly current offshore, the profile of large northerly swell was not there for the time being.

'The boys were certainly right about the water being opaque,' Louis observed and this morning the Garmin was showing a 71.5 degree temp. The satellite pics he studied the night before had not shown any anomalies up the line, no hook currents, bellies or eddy balls, only broad linear temperature changes that had the Gulf Stream boundaries exceptionally far offshore. 'Wish I had a marine biologist up here' the old dog thought, 'he could explain this all to me.' Louis knew the green water was far more nutrient rich than the bluer water, maybe some explosion of plankton or krill. He curtailed his analysis knowing it mattered little; it is what it is and the adjustments have been made.

The old captain put the boat on autopilot, and stepped away from the helm to get a better view of the morning sky looking up from the edge of the hard top. He scanned around to the east and then walked to the port side taking in the view to the west. "Bluebird sky like I have never seen," Louis observed glancing over at Emory, "not a cloud to be found anywhere."

"Like that all day yesterday too, Louie, same deal."

"Not surprised, really, surface map would have the center of this big High Pressure system moving right on top us today. We'll just have to see how things unfold this morning, cap."

When they arrived at their chosen starting point off Jupiter Inlet, Louis powered down and set the controls into their 'low idle' mode. Determining they could fish the spread straight at around five to five and a half knots, he then gazed at the wake as he was heading down sea, "No problem fishing her here, Emory, we'll do fine on two, we'll leave the trolling valves alone. I can always take one out of gear if need be."

"That's what I always do."

"Yesterday…did you see any birds sitting in the water when you first got here?"

"No, come to think of it, none all week for that matter. More than few here right now."

"Yeah…fish have more than likely worked the bait up at least once already, maybe at first light." Louis spied a clump of flying fish busting out of the corner of his eye off the port side. "Bunch just busted over there, don't think we'll have to wait too long."

Louis looked down at his watch eight twenty eight, "Two minutes."

"Lines in," Buccaneer Bob proclaimed via the radio tournament channel.

"Put 'em in the water," Emory hollered from above

Louis had the boat trolling down sea for the cockpit members to better set the spread without rocking and rolling. On the port side the Greek had his flat line pinned in place as Crafty was deploying his natural daisy chain of ballyhoo. He took the blue and white ballyhoo and observed its swimming performance before letting it back behind the boat, "Looks hot, Louie that hair does shine in this water" he yelled up as he was getting ready to pin the bait in the short rigger clip on the right side looking back.

"On the daisy chain, Crafty," Louis hollered from the bridge, "give her the rod." The sail was all over the teaser, flailing it from side to side, one time holding the last of the chain swimming off with it. Louis put the boat in a hard turn to starboard which helped the teaser chain to pull free and begin to speed up and skip on top. The sailfish then made a beeline to the short rigger bait now tended by Chrissy and inhaled it as he went to the side, immediately making a run away from the boat. Her thumb caressing the spool gave clear notice of the fish moving off at speed and she slowly brought the drag up to the button achieving rod bend and hookup. The fish continued to greyhound away from the boat.

Louis countered a turn back to port into the fishes track, leading the daisy chain in the opposite direction, "Tony, yank out the left rigger and bring it up behind the teaser and get set." The Greek did as he was told, but never quite cranked the bait all the way into the teaser when a second fish exploded from the green water and hoofed the ballyhoo as he reentered the sea. The Greek did well to feed him in an experienced transfer to free spool, the fish were eating quick and he soon found rod bend. They were now holding a double.

The mullet dredge was now incoming at the hands of Emory on the bridge as Crafty was clearing the daisy chain and hoisting it into the boat. He quickly eyed the last two ballyhoo in the daisy chain, or what was left of them, and immediately replaced the mauled creatures with fresh offerings. He looked at the long right 'rigger bait dangling from the clip, and could see it was also mangled. 'Another bite, two from three.'

Two anglers, two hot fish tail walking all over the place. They had already crossed twice but the Greek and his lady did the up and over flawlessly, correctly reading the distance and line from each fish.

Both anglers were making steady gains, and Louis would back mildly when the situation would allow. But the fish remained fairly social and did not separate in the way the old captain might have liked. They traded runs and soundings back and forth, neither one presenting an opening in which to be taken first. At last Chrissy's fish began to tire, and Louis turned his focus onto her sail to do an intercept in his backing down.

"Tony...we're going to try Chrissy's first, might want to back the drag off some especially if he runs off the boat." The plan fared well and Crafty put a knife to the leader three feet up from the bill, after first retrieving the blue and white sea witch. The Greek resumed cranking on his fish upping the drag, and Crafty took a look around to make sure he was ready to reset the spread when they disposed of the other fish. The teaser had been rebaited, and both long riggers and the lone short rigger had fresh offerings.

In the brief break he had, Crafty looked around the fleet and saw a number of boats doing battle. From a quick visual count he figured nearly all of the Gold Cup fleet to be in the area, but there was one rig that stood out. Flores eighty foot battlewagon was dead astern of them and they were also backing down on a fish. The Brothers Pride was close enough to the eighty foot Tribute for Crafty to recognize Adam Wendt cranking away at his sail with Flores standing behind him, perhaps offering his guest a little coaching.

"Tony's fish coming in steady now, Crafty."

When the leader was within grasp, Crafty extended his left arm and took a single wrap in attempt to retrieve the blue and white before cutting the leader. Under no excessive pressure the hook simply pulled from the sail, and giving the mate his whole rig back.

Immediately, Crafty deployed the daisy chain, and reset the spread starting with short rigger, then long riggers and finally mullet dredge and flat line.

"You got yourself a big sail there, Adam, fish would go at least eighty pounds. He's pulling a lot of drag, just stay with him, be patient," Flores coached from Wendt's left side. He'll stop running soon.

"Watch your backing, Doug, we're almost on top of him," Flores warned from below. "Hold up he's digging for the bottom. Take a break, Adam let him pull drag."

The Floridita was now dead in the water as the pair of anglers observed the outgoing line descending into the sea in a near vertical angle just a few feet off the boat. The sail had taken half the spool in his sounding, and even though the smaller diameter had added even more drag on the fish, line was still going out. Finally, the line coming off the reel slowed significantly.

"He is tiring now, Adam, let him stop before you try to gain back line."

"Think so, Henry… I think maybe a few pumps…"

"No…you'll just pull more line off the reel. He's got a lot of heat on him already; let him change direction before working on him."

The line finally stopped playing out upon which Adam Wendt launched right into a high arch lifting of the rod not noticing his tactic was pulling more line off the spool each time he raised the tip.

"Be patient my friend. Big fish, maybe foul hooked, a lot of drag, can you not hear the mono singing in the wind? It is close to the breaking point."

Wendt, by all observation, now appeared completely closed off from the world, and was not alert to the coaching of his partner. Once again, this man willed that he would have to take control of the situation according to his own comfort level, confident in his convictions. Wendt held the rod and leaned back against the fish providing maximum pressure of rod bend and reel drag, and line was still slowly sliding out. He looked down at the drag lever as it rested against the preset button, and he felt he could go over and beyond the button just a tad more. What he didn't execute was a smooth adjustment in first depressing the button before gingerly adding more pressure, and the lever itself popped too far ahead of the preset almost half way to full; it parted. "Broke him off, dammit!"

"Aiyeee," was all Flores could say as he looked at the suddenly limp line blowing in the wind.

"Think it was a knot?"

"A knot… look where the line parted," Flores observed. "We are only fishing tournament twenty pound test here;

Adam…you put too much heat on that fish. Capt. Doug will test the drag at the dock before he spools the reel. It is out of commission for the rest of the day."

"Sorry, Henry, I thought I had him coming."

"You should have listened to what I said…we'll get the next one." Flores continued to instruct and encourage his guest to avoid any further mishaps, but the experienced Cuban fisherman was already formulating judgements about his fishing partner. You can learn a lot about a man in these kinds of situations.

The fact that a bulk of the fleet had today decided to fish on top of one another had resulted in the highest morning catch of the tournament overall as forty four sails had already been released on the final day. Things were slowing down by eleven o'clock, and the radio had been fairly quiet for the last ten minutes.

Emory took a 360 scan of the sea concluding that the majority of fleets from three different inlets were now positioned from slightly north to slightly south off Jupiter Inlet. "Sure could use one more, Louie, there's a bunch of us with three today."

"One more would do the trick…for this morning. It's the afternoon I'm thinking about right now."

"I don't know cap, they haven't done much in the afternoon all week, and yesterday it was dead."

"I know, Emory. All these boats fishing on top of each other makes it even a bigger crapshoot…Kmart fishing. I'm going to move south to the edge of the fleet as I tend to believe things are all pushing that way. Getting way too crowded in this mess."

It was a little before noon when the bite died altogether, and the radio went silent. At twelve Buccaneer Bob gave the noon report; forty four fish today, six boats tied with three on the daily, Louis' team had the advantage of time over the other five.

Louis had continued his southerly tack for the last hour and by now had distanced himself from the congestion by a few miles. Somewhere a little to the south of the Juno Beach pier he spotted a charter boat he knew well, and picked up the VHF mike from its holder. Switching down to low power he keyed the transmit button, "Hey, Ruthie…., Charlie, y'on there?"

Louis watched as the captain on the bridge leaned over and grabbed the mike on his own vessel, "I'm here if you're there."

"Up two."

"Up two."

Y'on there, Charlie, Louis Gladding on your starboard side."

"Louis old buddy, how the hell are you doing?"

"Quite well, Charlie, life is good. Have you seen one lately?"

"Caught one from a double I was holding…about twenty minutes ago. That's it on sail, caught a real nice pair of dolphin earlier, bull will go at least forty. How about you, Louie, whatcha done for 'em?"

"Caught three from four before eleven, but things shut off up the road a little."

"Very nice. Stop by and have a cold one next time your down, we've got a lot of catching up to do."

"Count on it, Charlie. Going to keep pushing on down the beach, if I do anything I'll call you. Just go right to the one we're on now."

"Standing by. Good Luck."

Louis took a long scan of the horizon to the east only to find conditions had not changed much offshore. "Emory, you would prefer to win this thing, wouldn't you?"

"Absolutely…got a daily under our belt, and isn't that why we are here to begin with."

Louis chuckled a bit, "There isn't going to be an afternoon bite back there, and even if there was a small flurry, with that jammed up fleet our chances of seeing what we need are not good."

"Yes….."

"We were fishing in seventy one degree water this morning, and by the grace of God there were those flyers to keep the sails attention. But I will tell you this, I have many times seen sailfish feed in those extreme conditions, but I have never seen them hang around that kind of cold for very long. They do scatter horizontally as well as vertically."

"Go on."

"Do you trust me to make a move?"

"Already said that."

Louis called down to Crafty, "Bring 'em in, Crafty, we're going to make a run."

When everything was in, Louis put the Brothers Pride up on plane heading on a course of 135 degrees. Twenty minutes later he passed by some fresh blond Sargasso weed in about fifty fathoms of water. 'That's good' he thought to himself, not that far from some warmer water. Something drew his eye off to the southeast horizon, the very thing he had been searching for all morning. Maybe five, maybe six miles bearing 150 degrees off their position, Captain Louis noted a patch of Cumulus clouds only slightly behind the horizon. He gave her another hundred rpms.

They were south of the Breakers maybe almost to Boynton Inlet in 620 feet of water when they found the current push of 78 degree cobalt blue water. Sailfishing in 100 plus fathoms; extreme conditions call for extreme tactics. Louis gave the order to put 'em in and fish as he observed a few free jumping sailfish all flopping to the south. "Yup," he said out loud, "they have packed their bags."

Before Crafty could even get the last outrigger bait in place they had a lit up fish all over the daisy chain with a second sail trailing the dredge, his entire tail lit up in Day-Glo turquoise. For the next hour the creatures were all over the Brothers Pride like stink. Captain Louis let his folks catch six more before he picked up the mike, "Ruthie Charlie, go over."

Charlie was the first to arrive, and he finished out the afternoon for his charter in tall cotton catching four sails. Whether by Auto Directional Finder or radar, cellphone, or all of the above, Louis' position would eventually be discovered. After all, he had been keeping Buccaneer Bob fairly busy on the radio since one thirty.

At around two, the first boats began to defect from the morning bite and picked up and ran south. Then it seemed that everyone was booking it south, some down the edge, some to the southeast. When the faster rockets finally converged on the Brothers Pride and the Ruthie at a quarter till three, the fish appeared to be done for the day for all was quiet.

Emory, Crafty, Louie, Tony, Chrissy and the Omie Tillot named the Brothers Pride won the Gold Cup going away. They caught eleven that final day to finish out the tournament with twenty two sailfish releases for the four days. The old captain thoroughly enjoyed the ride home as he let the old girl do what she did best, cut through that head sea like a knife. He gave thanks many times over.

* * * * *

Crafty hadn't spoken a word since they left Singer Island for the awards banquet. He seemed to be in a trance, eyes straight ahead, hands on the wheel. Only once did he turn his gaze, glancing over at the mega yachts on the Australian docks as they crossed the bridge over to Palm Beach. When they had closed to within a mile of the Sailfish Club on the northwest side of the island he decided to run the playbook one last time.

"Emory, I can't thank you and the Greek enough for supporting me through all this mess that Louis and I have gotten wrapped up in. I very much appreciate the chat with all parties before we left the boat. I can guarantee you that Wendt will approach me with the worst of intentions, disguised by the most admirable display of good sportsmanship. Just remember if he comes over to our table I'm getting up ….to do something. I am really going to try to make contact with him away from our table if possible. Let's hope we can be convincing with our cover story."

"No worries, Crafty, this isn't exactly new territory for the Greek and the Gloves. They have their own collection of stories you might find very entertaining."

"I'm sure, Emory…don't really know exactly how this is going to play out. Just try to remember to keep Louis out of it."

The pair drove up to the club's entrance and turned the keys over to the valet before retrieving their sport coats from the back of the SUV. After Crafty helped his captain with his jacket they walked to the entrance of the club. They separated immediately once inside; Emory hunting out the boss' table, Crafty heading for the bar at the northern end of the club. The cocktail hour was in full swing with many guests already seated, drinking and sharing stories of the day's fishing and its eventual conclusion.

Crafty entered the bar and joined up with a few friends, crews mostly, who were sharing their thoughts on the day; views that might be somewhat different than those being expressed in the other room.

"Anejo and Coke," ordered the mate after brief eye contact with the bartender. They poured 'sailor class' toddies here at the club.

"Nice work, old timer," the compliment spoken from behind, "who would have thought?"

"Nice to be lucky, Frankie, and good going on second and on that daily by the way."

"Louis pulled that one out of his hat didn't he."

"How did you know it was Louis up there today?"

"Crafty…I saw him in those ridiculously close quarters. I also heard the change at 7:01."

"That's right…" good Crafty, " if anyone asks you though, it was Emory…OK?"

"Gotcha real fine. Hold on, man, here comes Flores and the man as we speak."

"See you later, Frankie, got to be alone for a while."

"Understood."

The mate slid immediately off the bar stool and walked to the corner of the bar room to study the Ernest Hemingway plaque that listed all past winning Captains of the Gold Cup. He overheard the voices of Flores and Wendt as they spoke with some of the crews while ordering drinks some distance away. With his back to the room he continued to study the names on the wall, hoping that he could engage the pair here and then finally be done with it. The private conversation between the pair was now getting a bit louder, and he readied himself for the meeting. 'play it nice, Crafty, relax,' still he wasn't prepared for the hand on the shoulder either.

"There he is…best damn cockpit man I ever fished with! Congratulations, Crafty, you guys put it on everybody today."

Crafty spun around to face his adversary sporting the biggest grin he could summon, "Thank you, Mr. Wendt, thanks a bunch. Just like old times at Chub Cay, we were lucky to stay on the meat, Sir.

"So humble you are…Henry Flores meet Crafty, a fishing partner from the Bahamas who helped us catch more than a few whites and blues over there."

"Crafty, I wish I had you on Floridita like so many years ago. I have known Crafty for many years Adam," replied Flores vigorously pumping the mate's hand. "Your Captain had a sixth sense today, and when you are first to the fish you are usually first at the envelope dealing! Did I not hear from one in the other room that your captain took a tumble last night? Hope he is all right."

"Henry, he's fine, and he still led the team from the bridge in all ways. He did the responsible thing and had me find another pair of hands to drive the boat as he was tightly wrapped up in a sling. I'll tell him you were thinking about him." At this confession Crafty quickly noted Wendt's interest in the conversation and was waiting for his input.

"I hope your captain….is it Emory, am I right, has a full recovery, and please congratulate him for me as well. Who did you find at such short notice; it appears he did an exceptional job today. Can you give me some contact info on him? I'm taking delivery of a seventy two Viking in May, and he sounds like a good place to start a search for her captain."

"You might call up to American Custom Yacht in Stuart

and ask for John Mack. He's not full time for anyone he's mostly a delivery captain, but very experienced in boat handling. I think you can catch up with him there. I would say, however, that I know he is headed for Costa Rica as we speak, but he should be back in a couple of weeks. I can give you a local number, but I don't know if it will work down there though."

"Thank you, Crafty, whatever you can do will help," replied Wendt handing him a business card, "I'll call up there in a couple of weeks to see if they can locate him for me. I would like to meet him and see if he might have an interest in running my boat."

Crafty scratched a fictitious number on the card and handed it back to Wendt. It struck the mate as funny how much Flores was studying Wendt with such focused eyes.

"The girls are probably wondering where we are, Adam. Nice catching up with you again, Crafty, don't be such a stranger to Palm Beach. Enjoy your evening."

The old mate began to relax a little as he made his way back to the bar ordering another round. Frankie was the first to buy him a drink out of the many crews who did exactly the same thereafter. By the time the surf and turf buffet had been announced, he was definitely in the warmth of a happy buzz.

Crafty correctly assessed his need for some food and made a meandering move into the buffet table area, loading his plate with lobster and prime rib. As he entered the dining room he scanned the various tables for his team mates as seating was optional. The mate and the Greek caught each other's eye at the same time, and the owner of the Brothers Pride waved him over to their table. Crafty hailed back and continued to search for the Flores table, and was soon relieved to find him at the opposite end of the room.

Crafty saw that the Club President and his wife had joined their table as was usually, but not always, his custom. The Pres was a competitor determined to learn the art of angling in the most scholarly pathways imaginable. He had a voracious appetite for fishing magazines, seminars, TV shows and anything that would enhance his skills to bring before the fish. Over time, however, he was never really able to summon his A game in tournaments, and those were the only times he would actually fish. 'He paid such little attention to the creatures,' Crafty always thought, 'he would even drop back to a great loop in the line with a third fifteen Mississippi count; kind of like a declawed Adam Wendt.' He had a good looking wife, though, he remembered from a past event; and she out fished him every time.

"Here is our cockpit ace," the Greek announced to the group, "great going today, Crafty."

"Thank you, boss. You know you and Chrissy batted .900 today on the bites, very impressive," The mate replied as he took a seat between The Gloves and Capt. Emory. He immediately went to work on the rib and tail before the table talk would take him off task. More drinks were coming and he prioritized his need to get some food in his gut. Gratefully, the folks let him dine quietly as the club President excused himself from the table in order to distribute the trophy awards and crew prize envelopes stuffed with cash. A few pictures were taken, and that part of the evening was over.

The Pres returned to the Greek's table, sat down and opened up the fish dialogue for the first time, "Emory…from the crew's perspective what was the key today for you and Crafty?"

"Well, Mr. Andrews, we were fortunate in finding some consistency early on even though we all knew it was going to be a challenging week with the influx of such cold water. So we just stuck to our guns and fished the same area all four days. It was no secret that the afternoon bite went steadily downhill with each passing day, until pretty much dying on day three. With everybody fleet fishing at close quarters today, we took a shot to hunt for some warmer water. We were well rewarded for our efforts, but I really don't think it was that much of a gamble." Crafty agreed with a nod of the head.

"We saw a few fish today," Andrews shot back, "but I just couldn't seem to get right on any of them. I jumped off both of my sails that I hooked, but Sally came through on her side of the cockpit and caught the only two we released. She's pretty good," he boasted, as he flashed a wink over to his young wife.

Crafty looked across the room and saw Wendt was getting ready to leave. The mate knew the man was going to eventually make one last pass at the table, if only to make an introduction and bring congrats, along with more questions of course.

"Sir, I believe you would have had better luck today had you treated your sailfish bites...[hiccup] more like white marlin, they were eating fast and weren't....[hiccup] staying with a bait that long," Crafty noted barely joining the conversation while still studying Wendt as he bid adieu to the Flores party.

"They did keep dropping the bait... I honestly couldn't get much of a feel of anything back there today; very, very frustrating."

Crafty continued to monitor Wendt's movement across the room as he made his indirect way towards the table, stopping occasionally to say good night to a few of the guests. Now he was on his way over smiling and waving at the Greek, Crafty quickly got to his feet and resumed his lecture to the table with a growing incoherency and notably unstable legs.

"Mr. Andrews...I...ah...[Hiccup] what I mean to say is... billfish are a lot like women...[hiccup] they all put it in their mouth but they don't all swal-" [Hiccup.]

"All right sailor, you have had your fun, we're going back to the boat," announced the Gloves as he easily gathered up and pressed the mate into a half hammerlock. "He'll be alright...too much fun for tonight," the Gloves declared with a smile as he physically directed the mate out, apologizing to the table members who by now were mostly laughing.

When they hit the parking lot Crafty looked back at the club entrance and saw Wendt standing outside the double doors, probably waiting for his car. Crafty knew they were being studied and he looked over at the Gloves giving him an imperceptible nod of the head.

It can always be worse. It wasn't a roundhouse or an uppercut, just a quick little jab to the side of the head. It was just enough to stagger the old mate as the Gloves carried him off into the night and out of sight of Adam Wendt.

Thirty minutes later the Greek's bodyguard deposited the partied out mate onto the salon couch inside the Brothers Pride, propped his head with a couple of throw pillows and placed a bottle of aspirin beside him on the teak table.

"This'll do for now, Crafty," the Gloves spoke out loud as he locked the double doors before stepping off.

* * * * * *

"Jim…Henry Flores."

"Good morning, Henry, let me take a stab at why you're calling."

Laughing at the other end Flores spoke after a moment or two, "The Californian has managed to once again find another hurdle to overcome. Doesn't seem like anything but a small bump in the road; I certainly hope you can lead him to see it that way."

"That's what I do, Henry, part of the landscape isn't it?"

"It is so old friend, but something in this newcomer causes me to worry. He seems to be a man too often willing to go against the grain. However, I have great confidence in your experience and judgement. If there is one who can settle things down and redirect things that man is you, Big Jim. Please see what you can do to maintain harmony and control."

"I'm expecting them at any moment, Henry. I have always been a team player and you can expect no less from me this morning. I'll let you know what transpires, sir."

"Very good…looking forward to hearing from you. Bye."

When Adam Wendt, his attorney and his primary land planner arrived at the Water Management Bureau it was a little before eleven. It was the second Monday following the wire of funds that formally cemented the Contract on their bid for the Aikens ranch. From here on out it was a go, the Due Diligence had expired and Wendt's syndicate went 'hard' on the deal to the tune of a non-returnable twenty million. Now their mission was to procure the entitlements from the state and county to take the massive project into Final Site Plan Approval for construction.

After they received the paperwork from Beach McDade by Fedex last Friday, Wendt's team had spent the better part of the weekend pouring over the documents in attempting to formulate a plan of action to best deal with this latest land mine. Although Jim McCravy had signed off on his end and was no longer directly involved with the deal, Wendt felt compelled to gather input from the big guy who had a long and storied experience with moving things forward in all phases of land development.

Things were pretty quiet around the conference table as the trio studied Big Jim as he read the recent disclosures and notifications from McDade. Occasionally, he would smile and look up at his guests over his readers with a brief eye contact; a couple of times he audibly laughed to himself as he jotted down a couple of notes. In ten minutes time he passed the paperwork back to Adam, took off his glasses and began to rub his eyes. McCravy began scratching his thinning hair as he stared out into space for a moment as he thought to frame his comments a final time.

"Well…," the big man opened trying hard to suppress his laughter, "I'm guilty of one thing. I seriously underestimated that old cracker."

"Can we dispense with the humor for the moment, Jim," A flushed Wendt fired back with a glare that could talk. "No one likes to be made a fool of in front of his people."

"As Mr. Wendt's lead attorney, I feel I have a strong case for improper disclosure in this matter, which of course would void this Contract and surely level judgements against any and all parties connected with this fraud. This broker or caretaker obviously knew exactly what was buried on the Aikens property, and for reasons completely unknown to me, used this undisclosed information to more than likely shop the deal to another buyer. "

"I'm sorry sir, again, you are….?"

"Arnold Rifkin, Mr. Wendt's Lead Counsel," the man answered as he flipped McCravy his embossed business card.

"Mr. Rifkin, if in fact these archaeological finds were unknown to Mr. McDade, there would be little in terms of a legal remedy available to your client. In real legal terms the burden of discovery in this matter is squarely on the Buyer[s] during their time allotted in doing their Due Diligence. The state requests all parties to formally sign off on these matters; which was the case here."

"Jim, Beach McDade had to have known all about this dinosaur shit, and I am convinced he was using it against me to shop the deal and recapture the previous buyers!" Wendt fired back, his face giving evidence of rising blood pressure.

"McDade grew up on that ranch, Adam. His father was the head foreman for forty years prior to Beach taking over the reins. Of course he knew dammit! But, even if you could prove it which I think would be extremely difficult, you and the former buyers failed in your due diligence to address the issue; you signed off on it."

"That would be the summation of your legal opinion, Mr. McCravy? I didn't know you were licensed to practice law in the state of Florida," Rifkin countered on behalf of his client.

"Mr. Rifkin…did you gentlemen come down here for an opinion, or are you just looking to ruffle my feathers and connect me to something? Over the years, I have dealt with enough mouthpieces to last me a lifetime. Now…just listen up for a minute, you folks are all overreacting to the situation. This disclosure might delay things for a period of time, but it doesn't derail the deal in any way. Adam, you've got the property, step one, but you have a long way to go in dealing with the state and Martin County. You can't even apply for a Land Use change with Tallahassee until next September. "

"Then, on to your work with the state on this Development of Regional Impact, and upon which the county will also have to rule on as well. Oh, and wait until you get into it with the county commission and all the intervenors on concurrency and environmental issues. As it stands, you're a long way from the Primary Service District, and well outside the Secondary Service district. Leaving impact fees aside, they're going to extract from you and your partners everything they can possibly get in granting you Final Site Plan Approval. They'll be arguing for water/sewer lines, schools, fire stations and maybe a package plant if need be. This is a huge project and it will take time and an effective team of land planners and attorneys to take it to final approval. The good news is that you can let the state ride roughshod all over your property now, while the important stuff is in the pipeline. If you play your cards right you could easily gain a lot of horizontal site prep and a bunch of fill at the state's expense. Doing things in such a proper manner has already been seen to benefit projects such as these with tax incentives and bond issues. Hell, this could all be a bad dream come September. Concurrency does have a plus side, gentlemen."

Adam Wendt leaned back in his chair and began to gather up the stack of paper lying before him, "Would you gentlemen mind if I met you down at the car, I would like a moment in private with Mr. McCravy."

"Not a problem, Adam."

The two stuffed everything into their briefcases and made their exit as Wendt accompanied them to the door, shaking their hands and closing it behind them. He chose not to sit down but slowly paced around the conference room for a minute to gather his thoughts. He stopped in front of a large window taking in the view for another minute before addressing McCravy with his backside.

"I suppose you're right to some extent, Jim, in your assessment of our timetable. It may in fact slow us down only a little."

"Your timetable, Adam."

"Yes…of course. I want to know more about Beach McDade, what can you tell me about him, anything…his family, his habits, likes and dislikes. Where does he live?"

"He comes from an old family who settled in the area long ago, much like my clan. The apple didn't fall far from the McDade tree as Beach was practically a clone of the old man. It was a natural for him to take over the reins of running the ranch for the Aikens. It took up a lot of his time, but he still managed to get a real estate license and dabble in some industrial properties over in Indiantown. He's done pretty well for himself, but I doubt you are going to be able to tie him to any unethical wrongdoing."

"What about family; married, single, brothers, sisters, girlfriends?"

"His father passed twenty years ago, he has one brother who lives alone over in Jensen Beach. I don't think Beach ever married, but he's no curmudgeon either. I've seen him around with some girlfriends. It's his brother that's the hermit; he lives a very quiet life of isolation on a piece that borders the Savannas State Park."

"I see…very interesting…Savannas State Park, that's in Jensen Beach isn't it?"

"Look, Adam, how you handle this little setback will ultimately determine the survival of your project, and quite possibly your very own health as well. In doing things in a right manner, it could greatly amplify your success, your public image and your wealth down the line. If you misstep ever so slightly, and bring the wrong kind of unwanted attention to the area, you may well pay with your own life. Are you hearing what I'm trying to tell you?"

"I have a lot of people and numerous assets at my disposal, Jim. I'm not so fixated on this McDade fellow that I can't see the value in instructing my people to deal with him openly and above board. Having said that, my partners in LA are putting a lot of pressure on me to make this thing go away as quickly as possible. They are not happy in having to unilaterally shoulder the burden of this additional carry with many answers still unknown."

"I understand your frustration, Adam, but now the state has been called in. Take my advice, sir, and let this problem fade away quietly and with minimal public attention. Don't let your personal drive and ego get in the way of the bigger picture. That kind of mindset might work miracles in the Magic Kingdom, but around here it will just wind up getting your ass killed. Open your eyes, Adam; you have no idea with whom you are dealing with."

Big Jim rose to his feet and walked out the door without saying another word.

One thing about Lake Worth Inlet on a moonless night, the lower you get to the water's surface the darker it gets. In spite of the numerous high rises, the Blue Heron Bridge and the stacks of the Port of Palm Beach all contributing a great deal of incandescence, there is almost enough light to create a sense of night blindness when one is quietly motoring around Peanut Island in a small boat.

Such was the case this night. The two men riding in the seventeen foot skiff propelled by a large salt water trolling motor were indistinguishable as they slowly cruised by Canonsport Marina at two a.m. carrying only an unlit working lamp along with a fourteen foot cast net that lay in the sole of the boat between them.

By all appearances, they looked no different than any other

bait fishermen who would be out and about at such an off hour working the top of the tide and the dark night to their best advantage. With practiced stealth they pulled up to the private dock where the Brothers Pride was tied up and secured the skiff to the outer piling. On this cold night in February, the two had prepared well, covered from head to toe in dark navy sweats and skull cap. They could move at will and be completely invisible against the dark ink that was a calm Lake Worth.

This was all a good thing for the two fishermen, for their planning and timing of this evening cruise had resulted in the best of all possible circumstances for their mission. It would not require much time, a quick entry and exit, a processing of their catch and then onto its final delivery.

In five minutes the pair was heading back north under the eastern trestles of the bridge with their catch completely enmeshed in the large cast net hidden by a dark tarp. The silence was as thick as the humidity and building fog. It was a little bit of a 'truck' up Lake Worth to where a much larger boat lay in wait to receive the fresh catch, but the payday made it all worthwhile. The catch would be quietly off- loaded to the sportfishing vessel through the transom tuna door. All would be secured and the bounty would be delivered to its intended destination still to be determined.

Bill McDade walked over to the front window of his bedroom and looked down to catch a glimpse of who was ringing the doorbell below. A man in partial uniform sporting a ball cap was looking around the grassless front yard, comparing his own surveying to something he was studying on the clip board he was carrying. On the third ring, McDade decided he'd better check the guy out even though visitations were a rare occurrence to his cedar shake and tin roof house at the top of the hill. As he made his way down the stairs from the open loft he was already questioning the timing of this visit. When he got to the door he peeked out for another quick look at the man wearing a khaki shirt and cap both highlighted by a 'State of Florida' logo.

"Yes, what I can I do for you?"

"Mr. William McDade?"

"That's right."

"Good Morning, David Maxwell, I'm with the Department of Environmental Protection, Bureau of Lands Acquisitions out of Orlando. How are you doing this morning, sir," replied the friendly young man. "Have you a moment…this shouldn't take too long. It's not official business, but I can assure you it's a matter that could be of great interest to you," Maxwell evenly stated as he handed McDade a few of his cards.

"Come in Mr. Maxwell," directed McDade as he studied the card, "can I get you a cup of coffee or something?"

"Kind of chilly this morning, a coffee sounds great, black is fine."

Pouring coffee for two, Billy returned to the big table and

nodded for Maxwell to sit.

"Well now that you have perked my interest, Mr. Maxwell, why would you come all the way from Orlando to visit me, with a park ranger living right next door?"

"That's a very good question, William."

"Bill."

"Well, Bill, I work in a completely different sector of the DEP. While park rangers tend to the everyday management of state lands such as the Savannas State Park, I am actively involved with the future acquisition of such lands primarily in the negotiating phase. Your property borders the savannas, and as such it is of strategic importance to us. I assume you are aware that we have already purchased some parcels to the south that we have added to the park. It is our philosophy that these pristine lands should be preserved and enjoyed by all Florida residents. That is our mission, Bill, and that is why I am here today to see if there is any interest on your part to see this beautiful piece go into conservancy someday."

"That's all very admirable, David, and I do support the state's mandate on conservation. However, I have no plans to sell the property any time soon."

"Of course... I'm not here to offer any kind of deal right now, but years from now you might very well chose to return this unspoiled land to the people. I would add that the state applies rigorous surveying and land appraisals always coming in at a higher than market offer; a plus for any heirs you would have down the line should you decide to take the property in this direction. We meet with virtually all property owners that are contiguous to state parks as a matter of course; you were next on my list."

"I see...it might come to that as I have no biological heirs save an older brother."

"My appraiser's map shows a free standing structure on the property, down the hill almost to the water. Is it livable?"

Bill chuckled a little, "Normally it might be, but it is so overgrown along with the access to it, I would need two weeks with a machete and chainsaw to clear it. Why do you ask?"

"It would seem to be a logical point of access to the water in terms of any future use. Funny, though, it looked to me like there was a clear path leading down away from this house."

"You run out of path pretty quick, David, everything grows fast and big around here; the scrub, the pepper trees, the gators, the Herons and the bass."

"No doubt, Bill, looking at that monster on your wall; and a four and half pound speckled perch. Good Lord! I'll just make a note for my files that the second structure is currently uninhabited. Is the structure sound however?"

"It is. You know Mr. Maxwell you might want to check in with the guy two lots over, he just purchased that place. He might be a little more motivated to sell and he has a partially constructed boat ramp on the property."

"Already have, Bill. Anyway, it was a pleasure meeting with you and when the time comes if you have any questions or should you decide to go forward in this matter, don't hesitate to call me. Thank you for your time and the coffee hit the spot." The young man checked his phone, stood and offered an outstretched hand to McDade before letting himself out the front door.

McDade watched the man leave until out of view and then went to the north side of the house where he saw Maxwell get into a white SUV with the Florida State DEP logo on the door. 'If it weren't for the coincidence of it all…it would probably amount to nothing,' McDade thought to himself. He was quite sure this was a very common inquiry as one of his neighbors had once spoken of it and attested to its formality. Unfortunately, that memory did little in easing the growing uneasiness in his gut. When Maxwell had been gone for half an hour, McDade decided to take a walk down the hill and let his guests in on everything that had just happened.

As he approached the cabin McDade discovered a number of things that did not look right to him. The fishing tackle was not on the front porch where it usually was and both doors were closed. He knocked on the door three times finally calling out for Louis before letting himself inside. The place was clean and spotless. The bed had been made with fresh linens and the small fridge had been cleaned and emptied save for a box of baking soda.

McDade was suddenly saddened and perplexed at the same time. What in hell was going on, there had been no warning of any kind. He thought Louis would have at least said something. He remained shell shocked for a few more minutes pacing and looking around the cabin trying to add some pieces to the puzzle with absolutely no success. He felt he needed to go up the hill and get hold of Beach to see if he could shed any light on the pair's whereabouts.

As he approached the front door to the cabin which lay opened against the inside wall, he instinctively looked behind it, if only to look at the only place he hadn't in searching the entire cabin. There behind the door, at eye level, an envelope had been tacked with Bill scrawled on it. He ripped the envelope from the door as his shaking hands fumbled somewhat in getting to the message inside. Finally he was able to open the letter, already somewhat relieved that at least his friends were alive.

"Hi, Billy, we are OK! We apologize for the sudden, unannounced exit, but the two of us just decided that this was the best way to ensure your safety, and Beach's as well. It would have made no sense to stay any longer, and telling you and Beach where we are going would have served nothing but possibly forcing you to have to perjure yourself. We have a plan and a destination we have put into motion, and I'm sorry that I cannot share that with you either. You'll just have to trust me for the time being my friend. This whole mess will, by God's hand, finally run its course and end. At that time we will all meet again in a much better place with all these woes put behind us. Cami and I send our love to you and Beach, and we are grateful for all that you have done for us in this time of need. Pray that we shall reunite soon.

Love Us

* * * * *

The unmarked black SUV pulled into the Greek's driveway at about eight am. A lone man in civilian clothes, save for the belt badge and the holstered Glock 45 exited the car and walked to the front door.

"Good Morning, sir, Detective Tom Noling, Palm Beach County's Sheriff's Office."

"Anthony Vecchio, come on in and I'll lead you out to the dock."

"We got the call around seven forty five…what time was it when you first went down to the boat Anthony?"

"Didn't have my phone on me but I would say it was around seven or so."

"What made you go down there so early in the morning?"

"Nothing in particular, I pretty much do the same thing every morning. I like to greet the day that way, looking for snook and tarpon around the dock, maybe watch the charter boats take off. It's how I enjoy my morning coffee."

"Was there anyone on the boat when you went inside, or did you not go aboard the vessel?"

"I knocked on the side of the boat a few times, but my mate did not answer. It was then that I went for the boat key to let myself in. There was nobody on board. One other thing, detective…the salon doors weren't totally closed, the boat was unlocked. That's what first upset me; it was like Crafty was just stepping outside but had planned to come back in."

"You mean he always locked himself in at night before retiring."

141

"Yes."

"Ok," the detective answered reaching for his cell phone. "Yeah, I'm here now meeting with the owner. When do you guys think you'll be here?" The officer waited for the answer and briefly looked up and studied the Greek, "Ok, I'll wait. Mr. Vecchio I'll have a Crime Scene Unit here in about twenty minutes, they're just wrapping up over across the bridge. Why don't you and I go up to the patio…I just have a few questions."

"Let's go, detective, I could use another cup."

The pair walked up and each took a seat at the patio table.

"Mr. Vecchio, you stated that the mate did not answer your repeated rapping on the boat, I'm assuming he stays on the boat is that right?"

"Correct. Currently, he fishes with us almost full time and I'm happy to let him use the boat for his living situation while here."

"Alright…I assume you have a good deal of tackle and electronics on the boat. Usually it is from the water that thieves plan a heist; how well do you know this mate?"

"I've known Crafty for years; hell, we just won the Gold Cup a couple of weeks ago down at the Sailfish Club. What exactly are you suggesting, detective?"

"Can I have this mate Crafty's full name."

"Radford Kraft, he's from Cape Hatteras on the outer banks of North Carolina. That's about all I can tell you about him personally, other than he is one hell of a world class fisherman."

"I'm not suggesting anything, Mr. Vecchio, just getting a little information. If there was, in fact, a robbery, we might want to know Mr. Kraft's whereabouts and that he is unharmed and ok.

"Absolutely…I can say without question, detective, that

Crafty would never directly or indirectly be part of any theft on my boat."

"Ok…and there has been no one else on the dock this morning at all; maid, fisherman, lawn crew, cleanup or sanitation people perhaps?"

"Nobody."

"You said that you first came down at around seven or so, yet you didn't call us until seven forty five. Why the delay, I would think you would have more concern for what might have happened?"

"I suppose it might seem I was little hesitant about all this, but I didn't notice the blood on the dock until the sun had come up a little. When I first saw the bloodstains, I didn't think it was anything out of the ordinary. If you only knew how many snook my mate has taken off that dock you'd probably report him to the Marine Patrol, although he does usually clean up after himself, but not always. I did get a little suspicious when I found the boat empty."

"You're quite sure it was empty?"

"I am…Crafty never slept anywhere but on that salon couch."

"That should do for now, Mr. Vecchio, let's wait and see what the Crime Scene boys can come up with. They should be here anytime now along with a road patrol car. Do you mind us parking in your driveway?"

"No problem."

It only took a couple of hours for the Sailfish Marina community to realize that something ugly had transpired across the way at the next dock to the north. The familiar yellow ribbon strung around the Brothers Pride and the dock was flapping in the breeze as crews, dock dwellers and the tourons all took time to stare and gaze at all the commotion going on over there.

Then it was the media and their jacked up sat dishes, preparing for the five o'clock news working the story from whatever info the sheriff's office was willing to divulge however minimal. "More on this story at eleven."

By the time the late news rolled out the headline, it hadn't changed much, "The Sheriff's office is still working the scene and our sources say they haven't pieced together all the evidence yet. Officially, they haven't ruled out robbery or homicide as of yet. We'll keep you abreast of this breaking story as details come in. Reporting live from Singer Island…."

Throughout the day special search announcements had been made over the airwaves, marine radios and social media regarding the unexplained disappearance of a Palm Beach charter boat mate by the name of Radford Kraft known popularly as 'Crafty.' The mate had many friends around the world in the blue water fishing community, and all were praying for a lead or a miracle that could help solve the mystery and hopefully locate the missing fisherman. None were forthcoming in the following days, however, and the fishing community was gearing up for a sad farewell.

* * * * * *

Louis and Cami smiled and made small talk about their future plans in buying a house up in Martin County, as they occasionally looked around at the rather bare room from the simple table they were seated at. One large mirror across from them was the only break in the gray paint; a scene from which they could both draw on from their past history as guests in the cop shop.

At the 'invitation' from the Palm Beach County Sheriff's Office, they had been summoned from the potential witness list given to the investigating officer by the Greek, to come down and make a statement. Given the voyeuristic nature of the setting the pair were certainly careful in their communication and choice of words.

"Morning, folks, I'm Detective Tom Noling," the slightly balding man announced as he entered the room, "I have been assigned to this case, and I appreciate you both coming down here to help me find some answers as to what's going on."

"Crafty was our close friend, Mr. Noling," Louis answered slowly.

"I gathered that from Mr. Vecchio who had nothing but a high regard for the two of you. He was quite proud of your victory in the Gold Cup and how much you both contributed to the outcome. According to my notes, Capt. Gladding, you were only on the boat the last day of the tournament, that right?"

"Yes sir."

"Once the boat was secured to Mr. Vecchio's dock, you then left to go back to Martin County right away. Why didn't you hang around for the party and celebration?"

"I was happy to fill in for Capt. Dillon, but it really wasn't my victory it was his, and I didn't want to intrude. Besides, Cami and I are trying to buy a small house in Stuart, and we wanted to see a place that was a 'for sale by owner.' There're not a lot homes available up there and we are tired of mooching off friends. You really have to move quickly if you want to score a deal."

"That's what I hear…it's nice up there …would kind of like to live there myself." The detective confessed as he picked up another file, "Camille…or Cami?"

"Cami is fine, sir."

"Cami are you and the captain married or in a relationship as they say?"

"Not yet, but we've set a date," The pretty blond replied looking over at Louis.

Even the detective lost his concentration for a brief moment; she had that way about her. Noling studied the second folder for the next ten minutes going back and forth among its pages exhibiting various facial expressions that defied an easy read. He set the folder down and rested his chin on his left hand and quietly studied the couple seated before him. It seemed he was hoping that one of them might speak up, but that was not the case.

"This mate Crafty…I would guess that you two have probably fished a lot of places over the years…that right captain?"

"We have…like I said, we are old friends and we make a good team when it comes to catching fish."

"I imagine you have your fair share of stories," Noling questioned with a wink, "like to share any of them?"

"If you are referring to the piracy off Cuba, it is the one episode I am trying to clear my memory of, sir," Louis answered deciding to cut through all the foreplay, "taking a bullet and having my mate get stabbed a few times is too high a price to pay for catching a winning marlin."

"Yet, you kind of landed on your feet with such a beautiful woman at your side, Captain Gladding." Noling observed with a raised brow. "She stated in this report that she originally joined the expedition as Frank Whitman's companion. How does all that get sorted out?"

"Detective," Cami jumped in, "Look…I was nothing more than a junked out stripper when Frank and his cronies strolled into the club one night. Why is anybody's guess, but somehow he took a rather paternal interest in me, and he expressed to me many times that he was very attracted to my plucky spirit. When I got out after four months of rehab, he then decided to give me the best, complete makeover that money could buy. He told me that now I am as pretty on the outside as I was on the inside. He often shared that he had a deep fondness for me, but he never laid a hand on me, not once. He was as sweet as a low flying 'angel.' I was for show and companionship, nothing more. Had I the time and opportunity to confess my love for Louis to Frank, he would have been ecstatic to the point of personally walking me down the aisle. He and Louis grew very close and had become the best of friends."

"Like I said, captain, you really landed on your feet. Well, given the condition of….let me see…the 53 foot Whiticar sport fishing vessel and its survivors and the statements taken from all parties, Monroe County decided to close the file on this one. Actually, it was only in their jurisdiction by default anyway, but I'm not quite ready to put this one to bed."

"I think you must have all our statements in that file, Detective Noling, I told the Marine Patrol and CBP everything I knew."

"Captain Gladding, off the record…please tell me how all this was pulled off and what exactly was the payoff?"

"It was, as I have already stated, a piracy from the inside out. There were other accomplices in a distant boat that were being given directions and waypoints to our location by the man who was holding me, my mate Crafty, Cami and Frank Whitman at gunpoint. That man was Scott Byrd. Mr. Whitman was losing his patience and something within moved him to charge Byrd who then fired a couple of rounds into Frank's thigh. He began to bleed quite heavily, and Byrd ordered Crafty to clean up the mess while it was still fresh. It was then that Crafty went into the side cubby to pull out some chemicals to clean up the blood. In so doing, he found our lip gaff and concealed it behind his forearm before walking back over alongside Frank, who no doubt could see the disguised weapon. Well…Frank was starting to go out or so it appeared, and he made an awkward final lunge at Byrd smothering the rifle between them. Frank was quite a large man, detective, and for the moment he was able to pin the rifle against Byrd's chest. In a second or two, Byrd finally pushed him off and put a few rounds in his head. Frank was jolted back and over the side he went. Before Byrd could recover, however, Crafty took his best shot and buried the three inch gaff into Byrd's right temple with the curved tip now exiting his right eyeball. In one motion he led Byrd by the gaff over the side, rifle and all, while getting stabbed by a knife in Byrd's one free hand."

"How did you three get away?"

"The chase boat had miscued on their navigation as they closed on our position, and piled up hard on the reef. We were able to get up on plane and run by them at speed out of view, steering the boat by using the remote auto pilot control. They hit us pretty good with a lot of automatic weapon fire and a couple of rocket grenades to boot. It should all be there in that folder, Detective Noling, along with pictures."

"They're in here, yes. Who was Byrd working for?

"The guys in the other boat obviously."

"That's one thing we can agree on," Noling replied sarcastically, "This man Byrd who worked for Whitman, what was the gain for him in all this?"

"They argued prior to any shots being fired, I had never seen Byrd so enraged. It could have been a kidnapping and ransom…maybe some kind of extortion or espionage. I just can't say for sure."

"What about this other guy, Wendt, he somehow managed to dodge all this crap. Could Byrd have been working for him?"

"Quite honestly both Crafty and I considered that, detective, but we had no actual proof of any connection to this piracy. We just couldn't say for sure."

"Why did you choose not to pursue the matter further, hire a private detective or go back to the feds?"

"With what exactly…what more did I have to give to the authorities? I'd said all I know, and detective…we both know that whoever Scott Byrd was working for is still out there. Crafty and I both decided to lay low and not make ourselves such easy targets."

"I can see your point there," Noling added dryly, "Okay, captain, thank you for being straight up with me. I guess the boys down in the keys were also satisfied with your story."

"Detective Noling, what if anything, can you tell us about our friend," Louis pleaded.

"Not much, captain, we don't have a body; we're still running some tests on the evidence. I'm sorry to say to you both it is beginning to look more like an accident, not a robbery or a homicide. That's about all I can tell you for now. I have to question a few more people; hopefully, they might shed some light or provide a new lead. In the interim, I would advise you both not to leave Martin County."

"We have no plans to go anywhere for the time being, detective. You have our cell numbers and that's the best way to get hold of us. If we score the house, I'll call in with the new address. Otherwise, you'll find us at the extended stay Holiday Inn at I95 and SR 76."

"Okay. Don't leave Florida, Captain Gladding. Thank you for coming in, we're done here for now."

Noling left the interrogation room and grabbed a coffee before heading down to the crime lab. He walked into the CSI's office and sat down from across his desk. His coworker was on the phone making some notes and the detective was content to let him complete the communication however much time it took.

"Tommy, let me walk you through this based on what we have up till now."

"Let's have it, Jack."

"We've got blood on the dock, blood on the side of the hull, a trail of blood on the covering board and a couple of spots inside the cockpit, my guess a splash from an external bump or force, and no blood whatsoever inside the boat, none. We got a near empty tumbler of diluted coca cola and rum on the teak table next to the salon couch, and alongside it a quart of Bacardi Anejo with about two inches of product left inside it. Nothing else is missing or in any disarray regarding the tackle on the boat and the electronics inside the salon and on the flybridge. There is clearly no sign of a forced entry. We have one Sperry flip flop boat sandal lying in the cockpit with the toe strap ripped completely from the sole of the sandal. Now for the clincher; we got good DNA from the glass and the bottle, and all the blood, and…it was all a perfect match. No other blood or DNA was found, and I seriously doubt there was a struggle of any kind. I think the mate was totally in his cups, tried to hop onto the dock to puke, piss or get some fresh air, didn't make it and took a bad tumble ripping off one of his sandals in the process. Or…he might have miscalculated jumping back on the boat after he relieved himself. In either scenario, he could have hit his head or face in any number of ways and possibly in more than one spot. He hit hard wherever it happened and that explains the couple of small spots inside the cockpit. Bottom line, now he is in the water, either out, starting to go out, or already dead."

"Where's the body then, Jack?"

"I checked the tide tables for that night, it was high slack about twelve straight up, and there was a new moon that always brings a stronger tidal current. Somewhere around two or three in the morning, that tide starts to ebb hard. Now, Tommy, you know how hard that tidal current runs south right through Sailfish Marina and wraps around the corner and out the inlet on even a normal ebbtide. The dockmaster showed me an occupancy chart for the marina that night and there were several unoccupied slips in the basin as well. It would be nothing for a body to pinball its way right out of the area and out the inlet. You might never recover a body if, in fact, he fell injured into the water. Another gruesome thought… there are a shitload of bull and tiger sharks right out front as is usually the case this time of year; ask any dive boat vendor. That's what I think went down, an accidental death either by trauma or drowning or both."

Detective Noling leaned back in his chair and quietly nodded as he considered the CSI's theory. A minute later he got up and headed for the door, "Starting to look that way…thanks a whole bunch, Jack."

Noling headed down to the garage and requested his ride. It was one o'clock in the afternoon, and his growling stomach reminded him he had skipped breakfast in all the running around of the morning. The thought of a piled high grouper sandwich really got the juices going, and he decided to head for the waterfront to satisfy his craving.

When he arrived at Sailfish Marina, the parking spaces were non-existent outside the services of a valet, even though it was the middle of the week. When he showed the young man his ID, he handed the courier his card, "Call me in an hour when the car is out front will you."

"Not a problem, officer."

No tables were to be had inside the marina eatery, so Noling took a seat at the corner of the bar.

"Want fries with that, sir?"

"Yes miss, please."

When the young bartender brought back the plate of grouper and fries she noticed the badge affixed on his belt. "I guess you're probably working on what happened to Crafty, You guys having any luck finding out what the hell happened to him?"

"Working on it, miss, chasing down a few leads, but nothing definite is being decided for the moment. Pretty sad isn't it."

"Crafty was extremely well liked and respected around here, everybody is bummed to the max."

"You always work the lunch shift or do you move around a little?"

"Depends…on a lot of things…staff, time of year, weather; you know the waterfront dining thing."

"I understand...but I would guess you still know most of the mates and captains around here, they probably all wander in here at all hours of day and night."

"Not really their favorite watering hole, but yes, I know most of them fairly well."

"Who would you say was Crafty's closest friend on the dock here?"

"Everybody was his friend like I said, but the guy who has known him the longest and probably been here the longest would be Frankie." The bartender than pointed out the window at a man standing in the cockpit of a boat, three slips down the main dock leading west from out front of the restaurant's boardwalk. "That's Frankie."

"Thanks...appreciate that young lady. This is a damn good fish sandwich, you know that."

"Can't go wrong with that here. Anything more I can get for you, detective?"

"That's it for me, you can bring the check."

Noling slid off the barstool and looked at his watch. He still had twenty minutes or so before hooking up with the valet, and he had a few questions to ask Capt. Frankie.

He donned his shades as he walked out and strolled down the dock to make an introduction. When he got to the back of the boat he took a private moment to gawk at its beauty and form, and its bristol condition. After all, he did like to fish out of his old Mako center console whenever he had the time.

"Spectacular vessel...beautiful, you keep her up in amazing fashion. Are you the captain?" Noling quietly asked.

"Yes sir, I am. Are you interested in going fishing with us, lots of cobia out there and a few sails as well...Frankie," the man replied walking to the transom from the tackle station.

"Nice to meet you, Frankie...no fishing, but maybe you could answer a few questions that might help me a bit... Detective

Tom Noling from the sheriff's office." Noling's response resulted in an immediate change of expression in the captain's face. "Very pretty boat you have there, captain, what is she?"

"A Rybovich... she's a good old girl, seen a lot of water under the keel in her forty years. You're working on that mess over there aren't you?"

"That's right, Frankie. I know a lot of the guys around here are pretty saddened by all this, but we're working it as best we can. Most people I've already talked to would say that you were one of his closest friends; had you noticed any changes in your buddy's behavior, habits, temperament, anything?"

"This year he's kept to himself quite a lot, I mean he's been staying on the Greek's boat most of the time. He hasn't hung around over here very much at all, not like him to be that way. The one time I jumped him and dragged him over to the Jetty Inn, he was throwing down the pops pretty good. I had a newbie captain riding along with us, and I wound up having to separate the two of them at the bar."

"Yeah... I heard that from someone else. Which boat does the newcomer skipper?"

"That Spencer boat docked right across from me. That rig hasn't moved in two months; never seen the owner or anyone get on or off her except the kid. He goes by the name of Danny...and I don't know anything more about him, and I don't really care to either. I'm sure they have some contact info in the office."

"Frankie, do you think Crafty was maybe sinking into a state of depression, some downward spiral that was possibly fueling his heavy drinking?"

"Maybe, officer...he was really in his cups at the Sailfish Club too...had to make a hasty retreat with his boss's bodyguard."

"Mr. Vecchio had also mentioned that to me."

"Look, detective, I'm not here to indict Crafty for anything, he's practically a brother to me. If you knew all the shit he has been going through this last couple of years you would probably understand."

"Been through… as in?"

"In all honesty, nobody really knows the whole story, sir, that's the problem."

"You're referring to the piracy?"

"Yes."

"Does that happen a lot out there?"

"It happens…you have to maintain your guard. Sometimes it's the boat, sometimes it's the airplane. Hell, there's been no small number of center consoles stolen in the islands in recent years."

"They don't hold much contraband."

"People have become as profitable as drugs in these times, detective, but then you would know that…pretty sad. Another friend of mine got pirated on his way to Chub Cay some years back by his charter for the week if you can believe that. They fished with him for a few days out of Lauderdale; all the while going thru the boat, taking pics and making duplicates of all the paperwork and other stuff. Following a fat tip they laid on the crew, the three guys said they had so much fun they wanted to try the Bahamas for a week. When they were three hours out, they pulled a gun on the mate and tied him to the fighting chair. Another one went to the bridge and held a gun on the captain. Amazingly, the crew got lucky when the captain dove off the bridge going around Gun Cay. The scumbags got so spooked they all took off in the life raft leaving the mate bobbing up and down adrift on the bank. He finally got free and swam all the way to Cat Cay. They got all three of those assholes; you just never know where it might come from. All of us around here are keeping our eyes and ears open, if we get downwind of something you'll be the second to know, detective."

"Frankie, I appreciate that, you've already given me some food for thought. I'll see you around, keep in touch."

Noling shook the captain's hand and paused to take a quick look at the vessel across the dock. Another beauty, perhaps a bit newer with less curves and varnished wood, but it held great sex appeal to the detective. 'When I win the lottery that will be me.' Noling made a note of the hailing port on the teak transom as he started walking back down the dock, 'Winter Park, Fl.'

The phone began to vibrate in his pocket, "Out front and ready to go, officer."

"Thanks mate, walking that way now."

"Mr. Wendt, Maxwell from DEP."

"Call me back on the other one, David."

"Yes sir. I met with McDade and he certainly wasn't ready to talk land conservancy any time soon. A super nice piece, though, on two parcels. Two lot splits and you could easily put four estates on the whole thing."

"Okay…was there another structure on the property down by the water?"

"Yes there was, Mr. Wendt. I borrowed Ranger Wilson's skiff prior to visiting Mr. McDade and took a quick run over there. There didn't appear to be anyone there at the time, but it's a very livable cabin in that it was clean and well maintained as if someone might be periodically staying there.

"I see…and how did you find William McDade as a potential seller?"

"He was friendly and he was not totally against possibly

selling down the line. He just wasn't quite ready to part with it. Something did strike me as being a little odd, sir."

"Yes, David?"

"Well…when I met with him I asked if it would be a bother to go down and take some pics and make a few notes about the lower cabin and the waterfront access. He said it would have to be another time as everything is all overgrown, and it would be next to impossible to get all the way down there. From what I've already told you, that was certainly not the case, and I could easily walk up the hill to within sight of the main house."

"Interesting…I suppose the old hermit isn't too keen on people poking their noses around his sanctuary; for once I can readily understand his sentiment. Keep up the good fieldwork, David, the time will come when we have farmed and collected enough pieces to go forward with our developmental plans. Keep me informed, and have the park ranger help monitor the situation."

"As always, sir, count on it."

"Mr. Wendt, I appreciate your taking the time out of your very busy day to come down here to answer a few questions. I know you are friends with Henry Flores as I am, and he felt that you might be of some help in unravelling the disappearance of this man Kraft. When I spoke with Henry the other day, he mentioned that you and he had fished the Gold Cup tournament together, but had been beaten by a better team headed by Anthony Vecchio."

"I guess everyone in Palm Beach knows Henry, detective…he is very much the true example of a man larger than life," a complimentary Adam Wendt replied. "How did you happen to ring him up, are you a fisherman too, like everyone else I've met around here?"

"I'm afraid I do suffer from the addiction, sir, and I am always trying to play catch up and get more time on the water. Actually, Mr. Wendt, Henry called me because he thought you might provide some background on Mr. Kraft as you had fished together before in the Bahamas. He said you appeared to be old friends who had caught a number of marlin together."

"That's all true, Detective Noling, Crafty was a good friend to me, and I am deeply saddened by this mystery surrounding his disappearance. He was an incredible fisherman with a kind heart, and was the consummate teacher in helping me to be a better angler. We are all hoping for a miracle that he will be found and be in good health."

"Those are kind words, Mr. Wendt; we are looking at every possible angle," Noling spoke as he picked up the file on his desk. "As someone who has spent some time with Mr. Kraft in relatively close quarters, would it be your opinion that he was a man whose drinking was starting to get the best of him?”

“Crafty liked his rum and cokes at the end of the day, detective, like most crews. I never saw it get in the way of his work, nor did I ever see him drunk until the other night at the Sailfish Club. Then again, it was a great win and everyone was buying him drinks. I was a little surprised, however, to see him escorted out by a large man at the end of the evening. That is all I can offer up regarding that.”

Noling opened the file in front of him and laid it out on the table in front of Wendt, “This trip to Cuba to fish that marlin tournament... weren’t you supposed to accompany the Whitman party as a co-angler? What happened that you never made it down to the island?”

Adam Wendt suddenly assumed the body language of a man who had suffered a great loss. “This is hard to talk about, detective, and a memory that is not easy to let go. Frank and I were good friends as well as fishing partners from time to time; his death at the hands of some pirate scum hit me pretty hard. Yes, our plan was to fish together in Cuba, but as the date approached Frank had to fly ahead via Nassau as I was getting loaded down with business issues. The night before I was to fly down, I took a nasty spill in the shower, and managed to wind up with a fairly bad concussion. On doctor’s orders I was advised to rest and cancel my commitment to fish.”

“I guess we could say you truly drew some lucky cards there, eh Mr. Wendt.”

“You could say that, detective, if that’s the way your blood runs. I, however, lost a good friend.”

“Sorry to be so impersonal, sir; I am only trying to get to the facts.”

"Of course that is your job, but the facts are that my going to Cuba was never etched in stone, and even if I was able to travel down for a day or two, I probably would not have been able to remain there for very long. There were work demands pressing on my schedule, and as it turned out providence ruled out the trip in its entirety."

"Did you have any business relationships with Mr. Whitman?"

"None…although Frank informally consulted with me from time to time on matters of life coaching and human resources. He was a true genius in the skill he demonstrated in building a company."

"Who was Scott Byrd?"

"Years ago Scott Byrd was once an administrative aide in my employ. With Frank's rise to prominence in the computer world through repeated product innovations and design, Mr. Byrd saw, and was offered by Frank, an opportunity to advance his own career. He had performed extremely well with me, and I completely supported his decision to move on. This is what I do in speaking and working with clients globally, as a motivational life coach. Frank was my friend. I was delighted that Scott would be expanding in his job description working at Whitman Technologies."

"Neither his body nor Mr. Whitman's were ever recovered; what do you think went down out there?"

"You're the detective you tell me. I knew Scott very well, and I'm sure he did everything in his power to protect Frank. He was a fiercely loyal young man."

"To whom I wonder," Noling questioned as he began to rifle through the pages and photos in the file folder. "What was the point of it all, Mr. Wendt, the piracy that is."

"I can only speculate, detective."

"You knew the only two people who didn't survive the assault, go ahead and take a shot at it."

"Kidnapping…ransom…" Wendt faded off and pulled out a handkerchief to dab the crocodile tears. "Sorry."

"Henry said you gave Mr. Kraft warm congrats the other night; how about the captain, have you seen him since this ordeal?"

"I have not seen Capt. Gladding since our last meeting at Ocean Reef prior to the Cuba trip, and whether I ever see him again is unimportant to me."

"Why is that, Mr. Wendt?"

"I simply wasn't as close to Capt. Gladding as I was to Crafty. It was the mate and I working the cockpit, and we became friends. The captain didn't speak much at all, and he always behaved in a distant manner towards me."

"Well…that is an evaluation more in keeping with your line of work isn't it, sir. I think we have hit on all I wanted to cover for today, Mr. Wendt, and I am truly sorry for your loss. However, I do think it would be judicious of you to remain in Florida for the near term, as I might want to question you again."

"I am deeply involved in development projects as we speak, and my plans will keep me here for some time to come."

"Very good," Noling replied as he stood and offered a handshake, "I will be in touch.

Wendt was just about out the door when the detective spoke.

"One last question, Mr. Wendt…you do call the Orlando area home is that correct?'

"I own a home there, yes. I also maintain a residence up in Lost Tree as well."

"Do you have any fishing buddies from Winter Park?"

"None that I can recall."

"Does the name Richard Demask ring a bell?"

"Why, yes…Richard and I sit on the Board of Directors of CalCan Corp."

"Mr. Demask has a very nice fishing boat docked at Sailfish Marina as we speak. I traced the vessel's document through the commercial officer down at Coast Guard District seven in Miami. Why is it that you were unable to remember him?"

"You know, detective, I've been so jammed up with this latest project I just forgot about Rich. Yes, he just bought that Spencer only last November. We have never actually fished together, but I sense that's going to change from here on out. I'll be taking delivery of my own vessel come May."

"Good Day then, Mr. Wendt. Make sure you're available in case I have a few more questions."

"I'm here to help in any way I can, Detective Noling."

Noling returned to his desk putting the files in his desk drawer before hailing his dispatcher, "Helen, can you patch me through to CBP down at Palm Beach International please."

"Right away, Thomas."

"US Customs and Border Protection, Agent Walker."

"Morning, Dan, Tom Noling from the sheriff's office."

"Tommy, how are things? What's shakin' up there on Singer Island, anything coming to light?"

"Not as of yet, Dan, still taking statements and waiting for some more test results, but I'd like a favor from you that might help on this one."

"Sure, Tom, what can I do?"

"I know it's a busy time of the year down there for you all, but if you get a moment do you think you could go over to the jet center and check their roster. I'm looking for a private jet registered to either an Adam Wendt or Richard Demask, or possibly a corporation called CalCan out of California. If you do ID it, I would like to know of any and all flight plans logged in the last three months, and more importantly, I would like to be kept abreast of any new flight plans submitted that might take the plane out of the country in the coming month or two. I know it's rather time consuming, but I have a feeling it might make something pop in this case."

"I'll see what I can find out right here, and I'll tell some of my guys around the hangars to keep their eyes open as well. We'll get working on it, Tommy; I'll be in touch as need be."

"Thanks, Dan, I owe you."

"Take me fishing when the dorados start showing up."

"Consider it done."

* * * * * *

Traffic was hardly an issue driving north on interstate seventy five at three in the morning. By the time the couple reached Valdosta, Georgia, the sun was just beginning to light up the eastern sky; a much appreciated lift needed by a sleepless Louis who had been driving for the last six hours. From experience, he knew once he got by the predawn hours his mental alertness would freshen and sharpen. The captain took a long chug of his coffee and started tapping his left foot to keep himself awake.

After checking into the extended stay inn in Stuart at three o'clock yesterday afternoon, he and Cami had proceeded to the rental agency where Cami was to pick up a car for the one way drop-off to Atlanta. Louis pulled over to the side of the rental agency, and gave his girl a quick kiss, "Okay, so you know how to get to Junior's car lot out on 76, just meet me there in about a half hour or whenever you get done here, and we'll take it from there."

"Don't worry, baby, I'll be along before you know it."

"Alright catch you there," Louis replied as he drove off.

As Cami was approaching the entrance, she noticed a good looking young man to her right as they both appeared to be equidistant from the door. She quickly decided to lag back and waved him to go in ahead of her, "You go ahead, it's all right I've got all day."

"Thanks, but you go ahead, I'm meeting someone here shortly," the man replied with a big smile, really you go."

"Thank you very much," responded Cami as she went to the front desk directly in front of the polite stranger.

"Yes, Ms.?"

164

"I have a reservation for a mid-size car with a drop off at Atlanta Hartsfield International in the name of Letourneau."

Yes, Ms. Letourneau, they're just bringing it around now; do you know about how long you will have the vehicle before dropping it off?"

"Not sure, yet, but I was quoted the daily rate with the addition of the drop off charge, probably a few days anyway."

"Whatever… you will get a break on the daily rate should you keep the vehicle for a week or more."

"Okay, sounds good, we're just not definite on our plans quite yet." Cami flipped the credit card and signed the paperwork.

"Everything is in order, Ms. Letourneau, let's just walk outside and check the car before you takeoff." The young man stepped out from behind the counter to review the car outside with Cami, "Sir, I'll just be a minute and we can get you squared away."

"Take your time I'm in no hurry," the young man replied as he answered his cell phone.

The rental agent watched as Cami exited the parking lot before going back inside only to find the lobby empty for the moment. He called over to his porter, "Jimmy, you see a guy with blond hair, he was just in line to get a car, and now I don't see him?"

"Yeah, he just walked outside talking on his phone."

"Hmm…I'll guess he'll be back.

Inside the small office Louis was finalizing his own paperwork and signing over the title to his truck to a longtime charter client, an old timer who chartered him at least twice a year to go snapper fishing around the full moons of May and June. Louis could have sold the Ford 150 anywhere in town as pickups, especially this model, were solid currency and always in demand. It's just that he knew for sure that Junior Bullis would be completely discreet in handling this deal.

Ready to move on, Louis and Cami returned to the motel and prepaid for the first week's stay. Around eleven that night they gathered up everything they had along with passports and plane tickets, and got on the road making way for Hartsfield International in Atlanta. They would not be back.

When you've been a target for as long as Louis and Cami have, you accept the demands of being on heightened alert whenever you stray out in public. You don't want paranoia to rule, but you become quite well practiced at sharpening your perceptions of situations and the people present within them. The pair had welcomed Bill McDade's invitation to seek rest and quietude at the cabin with open arms and weary hearts, but all good things come to an end in this world; it was time to once again shift gears. Louis looked forward to finally getting some sleep on the plane, but he knew full well that the 'alert mode' would be consuming him until that time.

Barring any major gridlock they had plenty of time to catch their one o'clock Delta flight, a nonstop; final destination Roatan Island, the largest of the three Bay islands thirty plus miles off the coast of Honduras. It was an island quite familiar to them both, each having their own personal history with the English speaking island nation, more Caribbean than Spanish.

Louis had been to Roatan a number of times, accompanying his adoptive Cuban father Alfie Silva on bonefishing expeditions hosted out of the Roatan Lodge on the eastern tip of the island at Port Royal Bay. He had stored some of the sweetest memories of his youth on those trips, as they formed and grew his love for the sea and fishing, leaving a troubled and truant youth far behind. Cami had done a stint for a few years working the cruise ships, dancing in the floor shows and taking advantage of any extracurricular activities that might come along.

The western portion of Roatan Island had undergone a massive port redevelopment, bringing in the shopping centers and nightlife that cruise lines are known for. But whatever the return trip to this island held for the couple, it would be a complete turnaround for each of them, with regard to their initial experiences of it.

Without incident Louis and Cami settled into their seats about twelve forty five. The plane was filled to the max, and there had been nothing to grab Louis' attention in any way that brought concern. When the pilot put the power to the 737 the old captain could finally close his eyes and take a break.

In what seemed like just a few seconds, Louis cracked an eye over to his gal who was staring out the window at the incredible mosaic of mostly blue, green and white that was the barrier reef of Belize below. "What do you think, Cami, beautiful stretch of ocean isn't it?"

"Louie it's exquisite! I always looked forward to Roatan when we made port there. The people were great, the shrimp and lobster were plentiful, and the diving…spectacular."

"You've never really talked much about your time down there, but I'm glad it's a place you'll like calling home for a while."

"My captain sweetie, I really don't care to dwell on the old days that much at all. I have never been happier, and I know we are doing the right thing even if we did promise that detective we weren't going to leave town. We're together and moving on to another beautiful change of scenery, and for that my love, I am eternally grateful."

"When I was a very young man living in Cuba, Alfie would bring his son and me to Roatan to go bonefishing on the most fertile, live coral flats I have ever waded on. There are some incredibly large specimens down there where ten pounders are commonplace. An English speaking island with a long history of pirates and black magic, it was an island far, far away; just getting there was a magic carpet ride all its own. We would fly a DC 7 down to San Pedro Sula and then jump on an old DC3 that had the windows you could crack open and look out. Some passengers even had some caged chickens they were ferrying back to the island. With all the noise and excitement of the trip, the birds would often get spooked, their ruffled feathers swirling around the cabin in the strong air currents; it was a crazy scene. Nothing separated the pilots from the passengers and you could see their every move as they made sharp banked turns from memory and dead reckoning, through the valleys around mountain tops much higher than your altitude. Then we would make a quick stop at La Ceiba on the coast before finally heading to the island; on descent, Cami, it looked as though we were going to crash on the side of a mountain, until at the last minute a dirt runway that looked about the size of a band aid appeared. That pilot made a landing of carrier quality, and when he rotated to taxi back to the shack, I don't think he had twenty yards left where the runway turned to reef." Louis was now smiling broadly in his narration, his eyes vividly projecting this memory for their souls.

"It will be fine, Honey!"

"I suppose so, Cami. We would hop off the plane and hike it over to the Coral Hotel for the night. The innkeeper, a retired Sgt. from the Canadian RAF, would always greet Alfie with a quart of his favorite rum and anything else he might require. In the morning, we jumped aboard a small ferry that made stops at many docks along the coast, on to French Harbor, Oak

Ridge and finally Port Royal, one of the many strongholds of the infamous pirate, Henry Morgan. Roatan Lodge was constructed on that very site on the western bluff overlooking Port Royal Bay. That's how the fishermen came and went; along with the mail twice a week."

The double tone preceded the announcement for the final descent into Roatan, and the 'honeymoon' couple fell into sync with the rest of the passengers buckling up and putting things away before the eventual deplaning.

Cami leaned her head on Louis' shoulder as she stroked his right hand softly, "It'll work out, honey, it just isn't going to be the way you remembered it."

"I know," was all the old captain could say staring out at nothing.

Big Jim felt reasonably assured in his handling of the situation created by the latest disclosures coming out of the Aikens Ranch, and their eventual repercussions both in Tallahassee and for the prospective buyers from California in the Wendt camp. He had consistently laid all his cards on the table, and in so doing had closed his part in the deal earning a very respectable compensation from the 'implied' contract. Never did McCravy assume, however, that his work in interfacing the Californians and the sugar people was complete. Fiefdoms like these, in the end, will always be at odds in competing for the favor of the people they so greatly helped install into political office. 'Like a good neighbor,' Big Jim will always be there.

As his driver turned into the Flores compound, McCravy knew the sugar baron had a specific reason for requesting a house call from the Executive Director. While this impromptu meeting could move in a number of different directions, Big Jim really had no idea what that 'direction' might be. However, through all the decades of power plays, and 'playing for time,' the big man had learned and mastered one thing above all others; know every conceivable direction and turn coming from the one sitting across the table, and provide the remedy for that particular someone whomever that might be. He would have to be on his game he suspected, but he felt he could successfully address any problem Flores would bring up.

When he entered the man cave of Henry Flores' study he found his host seated at his desk, browsing through a copy of one of Wendt's books. "Ah…hola Jim," came Flores' as he rose and walked in front of his desk to half hug the big man in their usual friendly embrace. "I have been boning up on correcting my personal inadequacies," Flores observed with a half-smile and an intended tone of sarcasm. He tossed the book a few feet back to the desk top. "Let's take a walk out back," he suggested with an outstretched arm.

The two men stepped out onto the terrazzo patio and beyond, slowly walking to the dune line and beach access well out of range of anyone inside or outside the mansion. The pair gazed out to sea for a time, each particular in their own way of taking in the view. McCravy committed to not breaking the silence.

"Jim… I am uncomfortable with this new neighbor you have brought into our world. Do you think you were able to reassure him that this setback will ultimately go away with a little coaching and some outside help?"

"I believe so, Henry. I made a strong case for his team cooperating, rather than seeking any legal retribution. He is getting some heat from his partners in LA, and their legal team would appear somewhat ready to chomp at the bit. If he accurately weighs the pros and cons with an open mind, I think he'll come around to a planned and sensible approach. I tried to present it to him as only a sample of the challenges to come. My sense is that he picked up on that."

"I'm afraid I was not so successful in getting through to him on even the most basic matters of instruction. In studying his 'manifesto,' I see a man...... wired for interpersonal disconnect and impulsivity. I have requested some additional background information from some friends; information that might illuminate a current mystery that is beginning to enlarge around us in this already uncertain time."

"Henry, I had my own discomfort about that too. I have confronted him a few times with my own assessment about what I believe he should be doing, rather than considering the weight of all his other options."

"Jim... a wise and powerful man is the one who accepts the inevitable; he makes his decision with the counsel of others, and moves on. A fool is forever in love with self, and sees nothing useful in the other. For now, Jim... let us give time a little more time. I want you to keep an old friend up to date on all that is going on with the Californian. I trust that you can do that for me?"

"We've gotten a lot done over the years working together, Henry, and that's not going to change any time soon."

The two men shook hands at the top of the beach line, before Big Jim walked back around the side of the house and to his waiting driver.

"Detective Nolin," Tommy droned after sticking the receiver between his shoulder and his ear.

"Tom...Henry Flores."

"Hello, Henry…I was just about to put in a call to you. I had an opportunity to speak to your fishing partner the other day; quite an extraordinary friend you have made there."

"I suppose so, Tom, he has certainly acquired a large following and readership with some of the more progressive thinkers of the day. I'm sure you've been following what he and his people are planning to bring into the area out to the northwest."

"I've been reading about it in the Post, but that kind of copy doesn't pass by on my side of the street very much. I did want to follow up with you to find out why you referred him to me concerning this investigation."

"Thomas, the blue water fishing community is still a relatively tight knit group, in spite of the tremendous growth the sport has gained from its media exposure and serialized stories. Mr. Wendt had spent a lot of time with Crafty over in Chub Cay and Ocean Reef; I simply thought he might bring a small piece to the puzzle."

"I found him forthcoming and willing to freely answer all my questions. His answers were all confirmed when I checked them out; I couldn't really add anything to what I already compiled on file here and from what Monroe County sent me."

"Tom, what have you learned about the captain who was also on board with Crafty both in Chub and in Cuba? He was the man Frank Whitman specifically chased after, and he was the one who made the whole Cuba thing go forward back then."

"Henry, you're referring to Louis Gladding?"

"Yes, we all knew him as Cuban Louie in the old days. An old friend, Alfredo Silva, had taken him in and raised him alongside his other son as one of his own. It was a wonderful thing and it stayed that way until just before the revolution. He and his brother and I were lucky to get out with whatever we could carry. Alfredo and I came to Miami while his brother decided to make haste for Tegucigalpa to help his partner with a car dealership they owned down there. Sorry to ramble on so, but see I'm giving you quite a history lesson."

"No problem, Henry, I find this to be a major bump in helping me sort all this out. Did you know that on the last day of the tournament you were beaten by an old salt on the bridge of the Brothers Pride that went by the name of Louis Gladding?"

"Hah! No I did not! Crafty told Wendt a totally different story that night at the Sailfish Club. I was studying the two of them very hard, Thomas, and I can tell you that I did not sense any closeness between them at all. That is one reason why I put you on to Mr. Wendt. Aieee…the Cuban Louie strikes me again…why am I not surprised. How did you find all this out?"

"Mr. Vecchio had supplied me with the names of everyone who had been on the boat in the last month. Henry, I had Captain Gladding in here a couple of days ago to answer some questions; he came in with a blond gal named Cami. They actually hooked up after the piracy went down off Cuba. Turns out that she was originally along as a personal escort for Whitman who was the owner of the pirated boat; you just can't make this stuff up. They were also very cooperative and I felt they were being as honest as they could be. They put it all on the table."

"Thomas, I don't want to take up any more of your time,

but I will leave you with this one thought," Flores paused for a good five seconds, "Find Cuban Louie, and you will find the one piece that makes everything fit together. For wherever he is…it will bring all parties together, and the judgement will then fall."

"Thanks for the heads up, Henry…I'll take that under advisement."

"Adios, Thomas."

Noling took the next few minutes to consider his conversation with Flores and the new lead that was extended at the end of the call. Finally, the beginning of a connection was taking shape; a thread between the captain, Flores and ….. 'That's the kicker' the detective thought to himself.

Noling reached into his desk drawer and pulled out the file sent over by Monroe County, and laid it open on his desk. He studied the pictures of the torn up sport fisherman that had survived the piracy along with the other three. 'Man look at the hole where there once was a salon window.' He looked over at the photo stat clipped to the photograph; it was the front page of a federally registered United States Documented Vessel. The fifty three foot Whiticar was owned by one Alfredo Silva, Duck Key, Marathon, Florida.

The detective remained like a deer in the headlights for all of three seconds before shaking his head from side to side, "Sometimes, Noling, I'm surprised they even bother to pay you for doing this job," was all that the detective could blurt out loud. He picked up the phone and made the call to the man in Duck Key whose phone was listed at the end of the report.

"Mr. Silva's residence," replied the broken English voice at the other end.

"Good Day, miss, would Mr. Silva be in? This is Detective Thomas Noling from the Palm Beach County Sheriff's Office. I am just following up on a piracy that happened awhile back; it will just be a few questions."

"If you hold I will see if he is awake from his nap, detective. Please a few minutes."

"Take your time miss, I will hold for Mr. Silva. It is important thank you very much."

"One moment."

It did take the better part of ten minutes before the weak voice at the other end responded, "Hello…..this is Mr. Silva."

"Mr. Silva, Detective Tom Noling from the Palm Beach County Sheriff's Office and I only need to ask you a couple of questions."

"Yes, Mr. Noling…. about the piracy is it not?"

"Yes sir it is. You are friends with Henrique Flores aren't you?"

"I am, sir… since we were both younger men. We spoke just last week, detective."

"He has told me that you took in a young man off the street, and that you raised him as if he were your own son."

"Then you would be talking about my Louis, sir."

"Yes, Captain Louis Gladding."

"It is so."

"Mr. Silva, in all the years of raising your son, was there a special place or memory that stands out in your mind, one that you both were quite fond of?"

"Well….we fished much off Cuba and Key West of course and the eastern islands, but….I think Roatan was special place for my sons and I."

"One last question, sir… Why did the Whitman party take your boat to Cuba? Didn't he own a sport fishing boat as well?"

"Si, is correct detective, but they had blown engine coming from Bahamas. My son, Louis, came to my house and asked to charter my Nina Mia. I would have given her to him, but he say he must charter. Okay."

"Thank you, Mr. Silva that is all I wanted to ask you at this time. I truly hope we can finally find out what really happened out there in the Florida Straits that afternoon and night, and you have been very helpful. Thank you for your time, Mr. Silva."

"De nada, sir….please let me know all that you find. My Louis is okay?"

"I will, Mr. Silva, I will, and Mr. Silva, Louis was in my office just the other day."

"Muy bien."

"He was in the company of a very attractive blond woman, and it appeared they were very happy you know, like in a relationship."

"So wonderful, Detective…Louis has been waiting for so long. You bring me such good news."

"Thought you might appreciate that, sir."

* * * * * *

'No phone calls on this one' Noling thought to himself as he was driving north on I95 headed for Stuart. He had that sinking feeling that the pair might have already slipped away in some fashion, but this contact was all he had to start with and he chose not to alert the two ahead of his visit.

He exited east at state road seventy six and made a right at the first light onto Lost River Rd, a frontage road that wound back south to the inn. He parked the SUV under the canopy entrance, and went immediately to the front desk where he produced his badge for the day hostess.

"Good Morning, miss, I believe you have a Louis Gladding registered here, would have probably taken a room a couple of days ago."

"Let's see, detective," replied the front desk gal as she went to her computer. "There is no record of a Gladding here in our registration."

"How about checking for the name Cami or possibly a Camille somebody. She would have been a very attractive blond woman who might have checked in with the older Mr. Gladding upon arrival"

"I remember her, sir….yes, Camille Letourneau that would be room twenty. They checked in about three in the afternoon a couple of days ago, and paid their first week stay. I personally have not seen them since that time."

"Would you have one of the house staff escort me back to their room. I would like to take a look inside the room or at least ask them some questions if they are in."

"Jeffery, mind the store for a few minutes while the detective and I go check out room twenty."

"Certainly, Ms. Salso."

When the pair reached the room they found a tag on the door requesting quiet and no cleaning or maid service. Noling rapped hard on the door a couple of times getting no response. "Open it please."

Except for one pillow propped up on one of the beds, the room appeared uninhabited; no luggage, all clean linens and towels, everything wrapped and sealed for initial use. At least now he knew, Noling privately lamented, "Miss, please do not make any mention of this to anyone whether they might be employed here or not. All you know is that they have paid up front and are registered guests here. That's it; can you do that for me?"

"I will see to it, officer."

"Thank you for your cooperation."

"Helen, it's Tom, I'm driving back from Stuart and I need you to drop what you're doing and get going on something. First, I want you to contact every rental car agency in Stuart, and see if they show any sales contract for a Camille Letourneau from 7:30am to 6pm two days ago. If you get a hit find out where the drop off was and what time of day or night. If you're lucky enough to get that far, plug that info into the nearest international airport, and check to see if there are any carriers that would service Roatan Island in the Bay Islands off Honduras."

"The Bay Islands you say, Tommy?"

"That's correct, Roatan is the largest of the three islands. It's also a cruise ship port at Cox'n Hole, and I want you to check their manifests as well. Time is of the essence, grab a civil deputy if you need to. I'm on my way in right now."

Noling entered his office around eleven in the morning and he went immediately to his desk to check for any messages. On top of his desk lay a stack of scanned documents sent over by Dan Walker from Customs and Border Protection with a cover letter, 'call me when you receive these.'

"Hey, Dan, Tom Noling…I'm only just now going through the stuff you sent over. Maybe you could condense it for me a little; I am chasing down a new lead at this end as well."

"It's all there in what I scanned and sent you. We got a hit on the plane, a Gulfstream IV registered to a CalCan Corp in Los Angeles. Actually, the plane is pretty well known around the jet center, a lot of splash with celebrities coming and going weekly. In the last three months all flight plans logged were between here and California, except for one trip over to Harbour Island, Eleuthera over Christmas. The plane has been sitting for the last month."

"Have any new flight plans been submitted lately?"

"That's why I wanted you to call me. The plane has filed a flight plan to Cancun, Ambergris Cay and finally on to Roatan Island for two weeks from yesterday. Evidently, the couple that flew to Harbour Island will be on board along with two other couples. Some of the guys remembered them; pretty well known soap stars and their spouses. They had talked of taking a really cool diving vacation if they could get the plane for the time slot. Well they got it, must be nice to move around in that kind of style."

"Good stuff, Dan…how about a Mr. Adam Wendt? Do you show him to be on the plane for this trip, or at any other time past or present?"

"Not on this upcoming international flight, Thomas, at least he's not on the manifest. I would say he was on many of the LA roundtrips in recent months, however."

"Thanks for all your help, Dan; things are starting to come together on this one. All I ask is that somebody in the field down there can meet that flight when it lands on Roatan. I want to know who gets off that plane, and I'd like the jet to be under surveillance for the whole time it's on the ground and the crew as well. I believe we might be looking at a very high profile homicide here."

"I think I can get that through for you, Tommy."
"Can't thank you enough, Dan. When and if we get lucky on this, you and I are going fishing on a classic old fishing boat. I know just the one."

"Now you're talking dirty, Tom, keep me informed."

Noling returned to his office after lunch at one thirty in the afternoon and found another file on his desk from his aide marked red. Helen had traced a car rental in the name of Camille Letourneau to the Enterprise dealership on US1 in Stuart. It had been taken out at three forty five two days ago with a drop off to be made at Hartsfield International, Atlanta. The car had been dropped off at the airport at nine am yesterday with no issues with the transaction. The Bay Islands were serviced by Delta Airlines out of Hartsfield and the first available flight out of Atlanta would have been the one o'clock nonstop to Roatan International. On the passenger manifest were Camille Letourneau and Louis Gladding.

"The trail is too warm," Noling said out loud, "almost a little too easy." Though he was happy to be linking a few things together in the case, the detective could not shake off the thought of how the captain might be laying a false trail for him; this one was an easy pick up. Or, considering the only other possibility, he wanted someone else to pick up the trail as well. In either case,

Noling was not about to back off on his requests from Customs and Border Protection. There were two unsolved deaths at sea at the hands of 'pirates,' and one related unsolved disappearance within his jurisdiction. He wanted things in place down there in case someone's plan was put into action. He wanted any extradition proceedings to go forward without a glitch. Hell, he wanted to find out if his hunch was right more than anything else.

By comparison to the cruise ship port, Roatan International was not high volume and space was at a premium, but the terminal was new, clean and a stark change since the first time Louis had flown in. The crowded plane had for the moment taxed customs and immigration to the max, and it would be a while before Louie and Cami would be joining up with their tour guide, Capt. Joe Gillen merchant marine retired.

The two men had been friends since first meeting in Florida decades ago. Gillen's duties of ferrying crews out to the oil rigs had required him to take up residence on the state's west coast on Anna Maria Island. They weren't able to get together as much as they would have liked, but there was at least two visits every year with each man driving the three hours on alternate holidays. The sea and the fish bonded their steadfast friendship like epoxy.

Fully stamped in and cleared, the pair moved into the adjoining baggage claim and picked up their sea bags before exiting the double door out to the curb. Louis heard a car horn and noted the flashing headlights of a small Toyota three cars back in the line. It was Gillen with slightly more hair and beard than he remembered.

"Louie you old bilge rat, how the hell are you!" Gillen had sprung from his ride leaving the car door open as he ran around the hood to bear hug his old friend, lifting him off the ground.

"Glad to be here Joe, and glad to see that you can still hoist this old man up. Thanks bud, for everything you have done in getting us settled in here," replied Louis. "Cami, say hello to Joe Gillen, the Mayor of Oak Ridge."

"Hi, Joe, we're so grateful for you helping us here, more

than you'll ever know."

"No worries, you'll make it up to me somehow, Cami," Gillen offered as he picked her up and planted a big one on her lips, "that is if I can get you away from Louis long enough."

"Don't think he won't try either, Cami."

"Now boys….I came down here to relax."

"We've got plenty of that to offer, Cami, here let me take your bag I'm blocking traffic," Joe responded, grabbing the two bags and throwing them in the back of the small SUV. Gillen led them out of the terminal and onto a well maintained two lane road. Louis looked over to the west of Cox'n Hole and saw the cruise ships and the port infrastructure that had grown dramatically to accommodate the larger ships and volume of passengers. Cox'n Hole itself had morphed into a colonnade of duty free shops, eateries and night clubs. The streets were jammed as Gillen picked his way through the city.

"A far cry from the last time you were here, eh cap?"

"I'magine…seen more people in the last five minutes than I would see in a couple of months," Louis observed staring out the window. "Is the whole island like this now, Joe?"

"Nah…it'll clear out a great deal by the time we reach French Harbor. We live on the eastern end along with the majority of residents. You won't see that much of a change from Oak Ridge and beyond. I'll tell you one thing, Louie; I can't believe your luck in scoring that house sitting job for Mrs. Jennings. Not two days after you told me you were coming, she calls me up for a recommendation on someone I trusted to look after things while she was in Bermuda. So you two got it made over in Port Royal until she gets back in the fall, and we'll all back you up if there's any problem. When I told her all about you she was completely all in for you guys staying there. Somebody be taking care of you, cap."

"Absolutely, Joe, been that way for quite a while; doesn't hurt to have good friends either. Does this road go all the way to Port Royal Bay?"

"That it does…sure makes things a lot easier around here. Jennings driveway is one of three that branch off from a cul-de-sac at the end. I know when you were last here; you had to go by boat pretty much everywhere east of French Harbor. A little of that kind of progress is okay wouldn't you say, Louis? Considering all that you have told me about this piracy, man, I'm feeling pretty good that you won't be isolated from the rest of us over in Oak Ridge. We can be there within ten minutes"

"I'm fine with that, Joe; I really am…this time around. Still got the divers working in the bay?"

"Different schools and museums come and go, but crews are still mapping and mining the wrecks. I think it's U. of South Florida here now working jointly with some salvage company from the mainland, don't really know that part of it. There are over a hundred and twenty wrecks in that bay, Cami. Most of the treasure's been long picked over, but they find a little gold or silver once in a great while. It's really a search about history and artifacts, deck cannons, hand blown rum bottles and amphora; no shortage of that stuff lying under water and buried around on land. They say the last real treasure find was found stashed in an old cave by the creek, not far from Ms. Jennings house. Story has it that an expatriated old Nazi found the cache near the top of the hill in a small rock cave. He shared his find with a couple of locals over where I live, and the three conspired to leave in the dead of night by boat for someplace, but the vessel was never found shortly after that. Most countries willingly split fifty-fifty; Honduras demands a seventy five-twenty five take, and the expatriated nazi said screw that. That's the rumor anyway."

"Capt. Joe...... the irony that Louie and I, ourselves piracy victims, are holing up in an historical pirate stronghold is one for a good story."

"One thing you'll discover and experience on this island, Cami, is a history jam up with pirate tales, voodoo and folk lore. You'd be amazed at some of the stuff people still talk about here in the banana republic. That's why I am glad we now have the road to be in closer proximity. We're only a two iron away, and coupled with the coconut telegraph we'll be able to keep track of everything going on around this end of the island."

Gillen now began his descent from the ridge line at the highest elevation of the island at 900 feet, and headed down towards Old Port Royal. The road soon ended in a cleared out cul-de-sac, offering three choices of graded rock and sand pebble driveway, each leading to a separate residence. Gillen took the southernmost of the three carved out roads surrounded by jungle canopy overhead, which in 100 yards would bring the party alongside the Jennings house. It was the first modern residence constructed in Old Port Royal.

In the classic Tudor design the house had the ideal view of the bay, and the cut in the reef structures leading out to the Straits of Honduras. The lodge's main room had two adjoining bedrooms and a kitchen, with one large bathroom and shower. Open air and screens provided outdoor access to a large stone patio which provided an unequaled view of the entire bay. A wooden stairway led down to the water from the patio to a simple dock, barren of any boats due to Ms. Jennings hiatus from the house. There had once been five hillside cabins spaced around the main house when originally constructed as a fishing lodge, but they had all slid into the bay from the deluge of back to back hurricanes in the 1970's.

Gillen caught Louis staring out at the bay and the few

other residences that had sprung up over the years, but had not really altered the face of the island here at the east end. Louis stopped and studied the large working vessel at anchor in the southeast part of the bay in the lee of the rocky spit that curled around to the reef opening.

"That's the dive ship and salvor's main residence down there, Louie. They do most of their supplying and shopping duties over in Oakridge with that tender. Every two weeks, a seaplane comes in with crew exchanges, and to pick up artifacts and any other 'finds.' Speaking of which, we got you guys a little stocked up for a few days, so you should be fine with consumables. I took the liberty of stashing a case of clear Nacionales in the fridge, Louie."

"Thank you my brother, you have made us feel very welcome. The fridge…I'm going to have to get used to having all this electricity and ease without hearing a noisy Bamford's Diesel generator clanking all day; running water without noise…now that is paradise. I remember when we had to put a new injector in the old girl during one stay, and the only fresh water to wash in was a little creek not far from here."

"Sounds like a romantic hideaway to get a nice bath, honey."

"The look of it was fine and the water clear and cool too. There was only one negative, Cami."

"Yes, cap?"

"Lots of leeches."

"Oooooo…"

"Look you two, if there's ever an issue with power we'll come get you. We have gensets for backup over in town; we're really contemporary here. Hold on Louie," Joe walked over to a desk and opened up the center drawer, "here's a Sprint GSM and a SIM card, use it for any reason you think necessary, we can always get new cards in town. I put a list of contact numbers for me and some friends, and all the municipal numbers in Guardiola. You might recognize the Police Chief by his last name, 'Belcirst.' Samuel Belcirst III."

"You're kidding right, Joe?"

Gillen laughed, "I did some research on the local constabulary when you were here way back in 1968, and the Commandant back then was Samuel Belcirst. His son followed in his command, and then his grandson the third is now the Police Chief of all Jose` Santos Guardiola. Look…I know it's been a long day; I'm taking off so you guys can relax and settle in. We are working on a car, but I am definitely coming back tomorrow by boat so as to take you two cruising and maybe a wet a line along the way. What do you say?"

"Sounds great, Joe, don't know what more I can say."

"Don't even try, Louie," Joe interjected before wrapping Louis up in a bear hug. "And as for you pretty lady, I expect you to live up to all the hype from Louie about your fishing prowess being amongst your many talents."

"As a charter boat captain's daughter, I don't plan on coming up short, cap'n Joe."

"I got no problem in believing that, remember…just a phone call away. See you guys about noon tomorrow, the tide will just be starting to come in then. Seeya."

"CalCan Orlando, how may I direct your call?"

"Good afternoon, this is Detective Thomas Noling from the Palm Beach County Sheriff's Office."

"Yes, detective, how may I be of assistance?"

"Is Adam Wendt in the office today?"

"He is not, but I can put you through to his personal secretary."

"Thank you that would be fine."

Noling went over the flight plan of Wendt's G4 again and noted that the plane would be heading for Roatan sometime next Monday, only four days away. Wendt remained off the list of passengers, and there hadn't been any changes to any of the dates or the flight plan itself. Another easy to spot coincidence… maybe, but Noling' curiosity eventually got the best of him. He felt compelled to qualify Wendt's whereabouts for the coming projected time frame.

"This is Brenda Waters, Mr. Wendt's personal secretary. What can I help you with, detective?"

"Ms. Waters, if you would be so kind as to inform Mr. Wendt that I need to speak with him at his earliest convenience. New details have come to light, and I may need him to identify some things, and possibly give a final statement. He'll know what it's all about; if he could call me by tomorrow, I would very much appreciate it."

"I will let him know immediately, detective; in fact, I think he is currently down in your part of the state."

"No hurry, but I do need to speak with him. Thank you and have a good day."

Noling hung up the phone and went back to the flight plan. The plane was scheduled to depart for the Yucatan early Monday morning, and eventually land on Roatan the following Wednesday. It was scheduled to return to Palm Beach International Thursday evening. According to CBP Agent Walker it was simply a quick loop to Cozumel, Belize and the Bay Islands. If that weren't ordinary enough, it was all about three young celebrities and their spouses on a diving vacation, island hopping on a private jet. 'This can't be anything critical to this case, can it?' After a few minutes Noling was awakened from his day dreaming.

"I have Adam Wendt on the line, detective."

"Go."

"Detective, Adam Wendt…I hope you have some good news for me."

"I'm afraid not, Mr. Wendt, not the news you were hoping to hear. We have found some articles of clothing we believe belonged to Mr. Kraft and other evidence that would lead us to conclude that he might have drowned. Would you be available to help identify these pieces and possibly make a final statement? We are almost to the point of closing this case."

After a long pause, "I'm so sorry to hear that…this has all been one total shock after another; all of it…so unbelievable. Of course, Detective Noling, I am here to help in any way I can. What do you require of me?"

"I'm not sure if it will be next Monday or Wednesday, but I'll try to give you as much notice as I can. Will you be in the area next week, and be available to come down here and make an ID on this stuff?"

"Certainly, I will be here most of next week in Palm Beach until Friday. Just ring Brenda up and she'll track me down; I do want to help."

"Thank you, sir; I'll do my best to give you some advance notice. I'll be in touch."

"I'll be expecting your call, detective. Bye."

"Good Lord, Noling, that isn't exactly what you wanted to hear," the perplexed detective uttered out loud in a moment of frustration. He reached for the phone to check with Customs and

Border Protection one last time. "Dan, Tom Noling, what time do you have that Gulfstream leaving for Cozumel on Monday?"

"Hold on, Tommy, give me a chance to go in to my office. Eddie, don't let these crates move from this spot until I get back," ordered Patrick as he walked off into the AC. He took a seat at his computer terminal where he proceeded to pull up the departure manifest for the following Monday out of Palm Beach International.

"That Gulfstream is scheduled for departure at eight thirty in the morning, Tom, six passengers and a crew of two; Cozumel, Ambergris Cay and finally Roatan on Wednesday. Apparently, they've added a day as they're not returning to Palm Beach until Friday. Then it's off to Los Angeles at two in the afternoon."

"No Adam Wendt?"

"Don't see his name on the list, at least not yet."

"Thanks, Dan, let me know of any changes."

"You got it."

* * * * * *

Noling was working on his third cup of unbelievably strong coffee perusing the morning edition of the Palm Beach Post when Adam Wendt entered his office at eleven am the following Monday. He was on the back page of section one finishing up on the op-ed piece laying out the pros and cons of the proposed Bio Tech Center now in the planning stages. The county and chamber of commerce were all in of course, but there were other issues of environmental and funding concerns being given a lot of attention by various groups; like who was really going to foot the bill and who stood to recoup the most money from the project. The area's taxpaying citizenry had been waltzed through these schemes a few times in recent years, and sentiment was running high that they had acquired enough scar tissue resulting from these underperforming 'municipal' investments.

"Good morning, Mr. Wendt, thanks for coming down, this shouldn't take up a lot of your time."

"This has all been a terrible tragedy…I just want it to be over."

"Yes, Mr. Wendt, I sincerely believe you on that. Come and take a walk and we'll head down to the evidence room. There really isn't much that we have; we simply would like you to state for the record that these personal articles were in some way recognizable to you as belonging to Mr. Kraft."

"I understand detective, lead the way."

The pair left the office and took the elevator down to the basement floor, past the crime lab and into a large room of categorized boxes. After checking with the file clerk he led Wendt to a large table and then returned with a box full of wrapped and sealed personal belongings, one by one pulling them out and laying them spread out on the table.

"One Sperry flip flop with a ripped out toe strap, one torn piece cotton t shirt with blood stains on it, one clean t shirt with Fishing Center logo on pocket, one unfinished bottle of Bacardi Anejo rum." Noling spread out his hands in front of Adam Wendt, "Look familiar, Mr. Wendt?"

"I'm afraid so…that was all I ever saw Crafty drink. He wore those sandals all day every day, and those shirts…I'm quite sure I have seen him in them."

"Good, I will just need you to sign an affidavit to that effect."

Noling packed everything back in the box and sealed the lid before returning it to the proper shelf. The two men made their way back to the detective's office where Noling's secretary had set some documents on his desk.

"Read the instructions carefully, Mr. Wendt, before signing and dating. Helen, would you please come in here and sign as witness, and notarize."

Wendt did perform a thorough read of the document, and in ten minutes time signed and dated it before handing it across to Noling. "There you have it detective, anything else?"

"Nope…I think that about covers it for you and me. You know when you walked in earlier I was reading all about the plans for this huge medical research center to be constructed out to the northwest just over the county line. I must say sir it sounds like quite an undertaking just in terms of financing, let alone the political ramifications and all those hurdles involved in the approval process."

"Detective Noling…at Cal Can we are quite proud of our

track record here in Florida. We have brought a great deal of clean development and sound business into the sunshine state. From well planned and engineered communities to leisure and recreational attractions, we have built a little something for everyone. More importantly, we all are about developing soft industries that complement the beauty of the state. It is our goal that everything we touch coalesces with the beautiful nature that Florida is known for."

"Bravely spoken, Mr. Wendt...I just hope the citizens don't get stuck with the bill or suffer any fiscal damage from the shortsightedness of a handful of business folk. Where do you go from here, sir, are you the captain of this ship who will be steering this thing from around from here for a while?"

"That's the consideration for the moment, at least until we get things shovel ready. I do have to fly out to California this coming Friday, however, to deliver a progress report to my people in Los Angeles.

"Is that right?"

"I've made arrangements to meet my plane at PBI as I'll be joining some guests returning from the Caribbean on a diving excursion."

"How about that now...what kind of plane do you own, Mr. Wendt?"

"CalCan is quite blessed to be able to afford a beautiful Gulfstream IV. I have let some actor friends have use of it for the week...I believe they left today, actually, for Cozumel. They were most appreciative and they all vowed to pay a fall visit to our interests in Orlando. Lovely people they are."

"The right crowd and no crowding is a very beautiful thing indeed," replied Noling flashing a wink. "I'm hoping you'll at least be around till Friday should something break in the case, you know, if I needed to get hold of you or something."

"Rest assured, detective, I'm in town until Friday afternoon and I'll be returning the following Monday. If you need me don't hesitate to call my secretary." Wendt quickly rose and stood to attention offering his handshake to the bewildered cop with that patented grin, "I was quite certain that you knew I owned a private jet, detective. Well, no matter… Cheers!"

* * * * * *

Gillen blew into the clearing beside the Jennings house in a cloud of dust and immediately began honking the horn of the Toyota RAV4. He was customarily early as it was a little before nine in the morning.

"Time to get up people, we are on a mission. It's Joseph and we have some fishing to do," Gillen clamored as he stepped into the great room staying pretty much by the sliders. "Where are you guys…come on you love birds arise! There's plenty of time for that, but right now we have been commissioned by BJ's Backyard to cater the afternoon jams with some fresh fish for the folks."

Louis soon emerged from the bedroom across the lodge clad in t shirt and skivvies, "Okay, Gillen, what did you have in mind?"

"Whatever is biting my friend, I was thinking of a nice fat wahoo if we're lucky. If not, we'll just hit the reef for whatever. Throw some shorts on and tell that babe of yours to get a move on. I'm going back out and wait by the car, don't want me beer to get warm."

"Give me five Joe, we'll be right there."

"Cool, I told the boys at the fish house to cull me a dozen good sized ballyhoo. I think we got everything else we need on my boat except more ice and beer of course. Get a move on now…I'll be waiting on you."

"We're coming, brother, just going to make a quick pot of coffee."

Five minutes became fifteen before the pair made it down to the car all dressed for fishing, and Gillen had the engine running before they got in. Off he sped into the jungle tunnel in another cloud of dust, driving like he knew every blind curve along the way.

"Joe, you're like a little kid who hasn't been to sea in a month," Louis observed.

"Actually, I haven't been out in a while, Louie, and it's not every day I get to go trolling with greatness and such a beautiful lady to bring us luck. Been looking forward to this day from the moment you said you was coming down. We're definitely going to slide a nice one in the boat, and then wile away the afternoon drinking to the music of the Backyard House Band."

"Sounds just right to me, Joe, kind of get to know everyone," Cami spoke from the back seat running her hands through Gillen's hair.

"Careful now, Miss Cami, I haven't even started serenading you yet."

"Don't tell me, Joe, you're the front man," Louis fixed his hat.

"You're looking at him!"

"Can't wait," Louis dryly added.

Gillen pulled into the fish house at Oak Ridge, and parked the Japanese jeep. He walked around to the rear and lifted the hatchback door, retrieving his cooler. Across the road was a small dock where Gillen's ancient Aquasport with a 135 Evinrude was tied up. "There's my girl, why don't you and Cami see what you can find in the tackle drawer, and I'll fetch the ice, beer and ballyhoo. Got an old 30 Penn International and a Shimano…hell, we'll just pull a couple of lines. Sound okay, Louie?"

"Sounds fine…it's all we need for a 'hoo."

"Meet you down there."

Louis and Cami headed across to the dock and jumped in Gillen's center console only to find the keys already in the ignition.

Louis hit the trim button to lower the outboard into the water, while Cami started combing through every compartment and side cubby in the boat. She opened the double cubby doors below the helm and hit pay dirt in the form of a plastic container containing hooks, trolling leads and egg sinkers, a skein of leader wire and some copper rigging wire; beside the case she found a small spool of 100lb test monofilament. Immediately Cami went to work assembling a couple of leaded ballyhoo rigs using a six foot section of wire and a couple ¾ oz. egg sinkers, finishing with a wrap of copper to seal the bill of the baitfish.

"Find everything ok there, mate," Gillen asked of the blond as he set the heavy cooler on the deck. He straightened up and looked over at Cami as she was finishing up the final haywire twist on the 2nd rig. He studied her briefly as she worked the tag end of her twist until it broke off cleanly leaving not a trace of a sharp burr. "You've done this before?"

"Got an arrow on this boat?"

"Afraid not, dear, got a little bait knife you can use though."

Cami went to the cooler and picked the lid up, "Nice looking bait, and perfect mediums for what we're doing, Joe."

"So glad you approve mate." Gillen rummaged through the lower compartment and retrieved the bait knife handing it over to Cami. She had filled a bucket with salt water and had the dozen baits soaking in it. She then started right in cutting out the eyes of the ballyhoo one by one. Gillen was taking this all in as he stared over her shoulder, and was just about to speak when Louis tapped him on the shoulder. Silently the old captain raised both hands and started shaking his head as if to say 'don't say a word.' Joe nodded going over to crank the engine, and after more than a few seconds of a smoky rich oil mixture they were headed out.

As they idled out of Oak Ridge Harbor Joe and Louis conversed about some of the changes that had reshaped the small fishing community. Occasionally, the two standing side by side behind the console would look back at Cami now stripping off bad surface line from each of the reels. The next time Gillen looked back she was tying Bimini Twist double lines, fitting an offshore knot to the swivels at the front side of the long leader. Joe looked over at Louis and just smiled shaking his head. He knew Louis had not been stretching the story when speaking of his girl's prowess.

As the boat cleared the cut on the offshore side of the reef, the water went from a gin clear turquoise to a deep gem-like indigo. The continental shelf or 'edge' does tend to drop off quickly in the Caribbean archipelagos, but nowhere is that more dramatic than in the Straits of Honduras. The drift or speed of the current in the straits is very strong and never ceases in its set to the west northwest. Thousands of years of this force of water has eroded the southern drop offs in the bay islands to the extent that there is little or no slope at all. Where the reef ends the profile of the drop off is seen in near vertical undercuts and dazzling sea walls. This sub surface structure is what attracts divers from all over the world to explore Roatan.

Tidal forces and the earth's rotation stack the western Atlantic and Caribbean Sea against the isthmus of Central America running through the Bay Islands, Belize and the Yucatan. This is the engine for the warm Gulf Stream current. This strong current flow is a critical part of the overall perfection in design that provides temperate and moderating ocean temperatures from the equator north to the higher latitudes. Without such interactions and the confluence of these warm and cold currents, the earth would not possibly be able to support the richness and diversity of life that we are all witness to on our blue planet.

In some breaks in this reef alone, the depth might go from sixty feet to thousands of feet straight down. Wahoo don't generally wander to far off the edge very much in their search for something to kill, except during the full moon of the spring spawning months.

"Whatcha' think Joe, like my double hook rig," Cami challenged holding up one for inspection about six inches from Gillen's face.

"Looks pretty clean, but will it swim, honey?"

"It will after I give it a little chiropractic, Gillen," Cami assured, now massaging the backbone of the ballyhoo forcing flesh away from the vertebrae. A few 's' shaped contortions applied to the fishes' length and the creature had become as limber as a strip of soft rubber under the shaking of the blonde's hand. She snapped it to the swivel tied to the lighter weight Shimano and let out the presentation back behind the boat, "Paddling like a champ, I'd eat it wouldn't you Joe?"

"Very pretty work, Cami."

"This should work well as a long back bait, but a planer would be nice for the deep line."

"No planer, but there should be a 12 oz. trolling lead somewhere in the-"

"I found one, though I kind of prefer the planer for the hookup. I took this old red and black skirt and slid it down over this bait for the down line." Cami then snapped the cigar lead to the Penn Int'l 30, tying a 50 foot section of the 100 pound mono to the other end for an extended leader and then another final snap swivel for the wire rigged bait at the end of the of 100 pound mono. "I like this presentation as much as any other, it sure caught dad and I a lot of wahoo over the years in the Bahamas. Well we got baits in the water, we be fishing. All you have to do now, Joe, is drive over a couple of them."

"Pressure's on, Cami…going to troll up current east back toward Port Royal for an hour, then down sea it home at a little faster speed. Let sees what we catches."

Captain Joe pretty much paralleled the color change about 20 feet into the indigo offshore side of the drop, only making slight turns along the tack to alter the depths and the speed of the two baits. By the time they reached the opening into Port Royal Bay at the reef cut, they had only been jumped by a couple of barracuda, releasing one pretty good specimen of thirty pounds. Gillen fanned a fresh bait spread around the opening before heading back down sea towards home, "I think now I'll bump it up a couple of hundred rpm or so."

About half way back they trolled by a very thick area of large coral heads that joined a bonefish flat to the outer drop, and Gillen made a sharp turn into them, and then countered back out dropping the baits. The deep line found immediate rod bend and the tip started shaking as heavy drag was now being run off the reel at very high speed. Suddenly, way behind the boat, the top line bait disappeared in an explosion of white water at the crash of the second wahoo. The clickers on both reels were screaming under the speed of the fishes' initial runs, and though both rods were bent over they were still shaking at the tip from creatures' vicious attack and all the head shaking going on beneath the surface.

"Double header wahooie from that angry mob," Cami yelled, "grab 'em, boys I'll wire and stroke them for you!"

The two captains came to there senses, conceding that Cami was now officially in charge; each went for a rod. The clickers were turned off, and the two men were now engaged in a battle with the tables turned. They were not piloting from the bridge or shouting instructions; in a rare cameo they had now become the designated crankers.

Louis probably had on the smaller of the two, and he didn't have the extra challenge of a heavy lead between him and the fish. It was coming to the boat much sooner than Joe's and the fishes' neon lateral bars were now lighting up the purple water like day-glow thirty feet behind the boat.

Cami had the boat idling ahead and away from the drop to allow her to leave the wheel and grab the leader with her glove hand and prepare to make the gaff. Louis quick pumped the fish to within eight feet of the stern and then walked back from the gunnel to let Cami slip in front of him and take a wrap. She made a good head shot on the first attempt and lifted the 35 pound wahoo into Gillen's cooler before slamming and sitting on the lid.

"Nice shooting, baby, liked that," Louis smiled over at her.

"Thanks honey, but I want you to stroke the other one…nice big fish, long leader, and he just made his third run off the boat."

"I got it; I got it…stay with him, Joe, and pass the lead over to Cami when it's doable."

"No worries, Louie, this one's going to be butterflied for the barbie."

Another couple of drag-pulling runs were made by the big wahoo until it seemed like it might be ready to come into the boat. Cami grabbed the big cigar lead and handed back to Joe, "Ok, Joe, just walk back a little, I'll start wiring this bad boy in, and if you can keep those discarded coils sorted out just in case. This one's got some girth, see him all lit up back there." In the next moment Cami saw the six foot fish spin away on a strong kick which immediately outstretched her arms to their limit and she wisely dumped the mono leader as the fish made yet another long high speed run off the boat. Gillen leaned and leveraged on the bent over rod and let the creature run and pull drag until tiring.

"Sorry, Joe I didn't want to bust him off. You got him coming again-we're almost ready to start over."

Once again she was gaining back mono nicely. Fifty feet is a lot of leader, and a lot can go wrong with wahoo at the boat. The six foot long fish was now a few feet subsurface only ten feet back. 'Fat girthy fish she thought to herself, steady but smooth, no snatching, no pressure changes,' and then suddenly the fish kicked hard and his head and teeth exploded from the water, his gills shaking and extending out to rid himself of the hook. Cami dropped both hands down near the water and dumped some leader back to the fish as he kicked and again swam away from the boat. The release of some pressure had its effect and the creature settled down, led again in a slow swim toward the boat. She started to take wraps and gain leader once more, finally presenting the fish just a few feet behind and away from the stern of the boat. She slowly walked back in a two handed wrap, "Louie."

All she saw was the flash of steel as the staff came forward along the fishes back until the gaff found home behind the gill, as water and blood was suddenly spraying everywhere. Louis, with some degree of difficulty, did not cease in his motion as he continued to haul the big wahoo over the gunnel onto the deck, "Give this bad boy some room and watch those teeth!"

The three just went forward for a bit, and let the twisting and biting creature have its way. In a few minutes the movements became less intense and more spread apart until the lateral bars brilliantly glowed a final time, and the fish passed. The two men and the girl hugged one another happy as could be before Joe made the initial assessment, "That one will go 80."

"Easy," the blond lady added.

"Take a load off, Fannie…F, C, Bf
"Take a load for free…F, C, Bf
"Take a load off, Fannie…F, C, Bf
"And put the load…put the load…put the load right on me…F, C, Dm, C, Bf once more for good measure…

The Backyard House band concluded their rendition of the ever popular Band favorite from the Big Pink album right down to the four part harmony. The group was then solidly rewarded with assorted hoots and thunderous applause.

"Thanks everybody, we really like to hear that stuff, now grab some more fish off the grill, get you some cold beer and chow down; got plenty. Me and the lads are going to take a little break, and grab some refreshment ourselves. We'll be back in a while."

Gillen set the old Fender on his stand and switched his amp to standby before joining Louis seated alone at a front table.

"Joe…considering what you boys got to work with down here y' all put out a pretty good sound. I really hate to admit this, bud, but you can actually sing half bad."

"Thanks, Louis, for those heart-rending thoughts," Gillen answered with a smile, "been working on it a little bit, but know we're not quite ready for the studio just yet."

"Seriously, Joe, I didn't think you had it in you."

"The folks love it and that's all that really matters down here. We expats are living large and loving life. Every day is a joy, and we all look after one another here on Roatan. You and Cami should think seriously about moving down here permanently as much as you talk about your fond memories of this place."

"Maybe, that will happen, Joe…kind of hard to plan for the future at least until our circumstances get sorted out."

"I know, Louie, sure is a crappy deal…all this damn drama dragging on day after day. I'll say one thing, good buddy…she makes it all worthwhile." Gillen expressed as he glanced out at Cami leaning on the veranda railing. She was enjoying the cool breeze as she gazed out at the Straights of Honduras and beyond. She certainly appeared at ease, she had been taking in the view for the better part of an hour. "Cuban Louie you be a very lucky man. I only say that because someone like that has eluded me all my life, but then you already know that."

"Wasn't it you that said life is a banquet and I have a fork in each hand. Yes I am lucky to have a woman like Cami come into my life, as blessed as any man could ever hope to be. It wasn't always like that for me for a long time though…or her for that matter. She's been through some stuff, Joe…done her share of penance along the way trying to keep her distance from that grave that once stared at her."

"She's some kind of infectious. Louie, she gets a real kick out of life. She's a very pretty lady and she's got a great spirit."

"Through and through, Joe… just love her more than anything. Every moment we spend together is precious to me." Louis quietly looked over to his girl and smiled briefly, "Once we were two people each loaded down with a very checkered history; two adventurers who had pretty much run the table on self-reliance. Through years of isolation and denial, and finally hitting bottom, we both came to the realization that we had built a pretty strong and impenetrable wall of solitary confinement. One day by grace, by completely undeserved favor if you will, we were led out of that prison by something far greater than our own wants and motives. We hadn't known each other yet, but since meeting we have often talked about this; we both knew something began working in our lives that gave us a new strength to change our ways. It wasn't our timing or planning or even willpower that energized us, thankfully, or we probably would never have met. Joe, I tend to think that's why you and I took to the sea so much. There was so much life, beauty, power and majesty out there it couldn't help but make you feel small and insignificant."

"It certainly had that effect on me, Louie."

"Yeah…Cami and I share together and rejoice in that bond as well. We delight in one another, and in all that we are not as individuals. Strange isn't it my brother that we find more peace and understanding from those things handed down to us from outside our experience and determination. One dark and lonely day years ago a Spirit began a good work in me. He came to me for I can honestly say I did not search Him out. He spoke the truth about me and my condition, and He began to reveal exactly who He was. He showed me His love and good purpose for my life in everything I saw around me. Over time I began to love the Giver rather than the gift, the Creator not just the creation and creature. Joe ask yourself….what is all that is good and satisfying in this life that we did not receive? As you have just said your love for one another here on the island, and the fact that you all look out for each other satisfies the soul like no other."

"Tell it cap, that's why we all want you and Cami to stick around."

"We are working on it, and we both do love it here, but let me just say this one time to be clear, Joe. When you hear that voice speaking directly to you, receive it as a gift and give thanks. This will be the beginning of true wisdom which comes from the heart not the mind. The Good Shepherd has said that his sheep know his voice, and that he is with them always. He will nourish and care for your soul in ways that are probably unimaginable to you right now."

Gillen appeared quite moved by his friend's thoughts and he seemed to be measuring his own words in how to respond. He nodded in assent slowly and quietly, but could not get them out for the moment. "All good there, Louie, but how does this square with all the trouble raining down on you two all this time?"

"This is a fallen world, Joe, there is clearly much evil to be seen in it, and that is not going to change until the end of this age. But know this…it does not change one thing I have told you about the Spirit who alone is true and incapable of doing evil. He is with you always as a joyous redeemer in good and hard times; therein is His Glory and the Victory is truly all His. He has given and worked in me the faith to trust in Him alone."

"I have been thinking about these things, Louie, more and more as the years roll on. I just hope what we're doing-"

Gillen cut his sentence short as Cami began walking over to the table and he flashed her a big smile, "You like my serenade you corn silk beauty?"

"Positively warmed my heart, Joey, you really got it going on!"

"That's it…no other stirrings?"

"Oh stop it sailor," she scolded him before giving him a big hug and kiss.

The fading light had not altered in any way the steady, soothing coolness of the ten knot trade winds moving gently across the bay. The honeymooners were reclining on the very comfortable double wide chaise Mrs. Jennings had commissioned for the outside terrace. In a peaceful embrace Cami lay within Louis' outstretched arms as they gazed at the daylight's retreat. Second by second, the backlight of sunset exchanged places with the ever darkening curtain of night. One by one, the stars emerged according to their assigned brightness and size in their orderly time of arrival. On this night of the new moon, there would be no heavenly spot light or any other indirect shore light restricting their viewing. When the day had fully transferred its light unto the night, the pair had found themselves in a sea of stars and star beams reflecting off the calm water. So many stars now visible in the heavens, they had actually disguised the more familiar constellations causing them to appear less discernible; they were not just observing the night sky, they were ascending up into it.

"My God, Louis…I have never seen so many stars in the heavens as I am seeing tonight, and the way they are reflecting off the water, well…seen plenty of moonbeams but never anything quite as overwhelming as this. I feel like I am floating, rising high up into the night sky; like I'm in heaven maybe."

"The Lord displays His presence, majesty and love over all, even in his provision for the darkness. He who rules over creation gives light to the night, and stamps that truth deep within the heart of every man and woman. Praise Him, Cami," was all Louis could say further as he tightened his arms around his woman. "Look at the horizon to the south where the Milky Way is smeared across the sky, the southern cross is just starting its climb up."

"I see it, honey," Cami replied as she stroked the arms of her captain that held her firmly in a loving embrace. "How high up from the horizon will the cross rise, honey? Louis…hello… oh Louie?"

A very long day's journey into night had finally overtaken the older captain and had blanketed him in peace.

"It's been a long day covering a lot of ground, my love. Let's go to bed. Here… I'll give you a hand."

* * * * * *

Louis began his stirring at the pink light of early dawn as was his lifelong habit. He put on his skivvies and walked over to the pantry by the simple kitchen in search of some coffee and a percolator. He was delighted to find some fresh Honduran and soon it would provide a fine roast brewed specifically strong to get his day going.

He stretched slowly spreading his arms and swaying his back to the sounds of more than a few pops and crackles. A life at sea will eventually beat down the body of even the heartiest of souls, but that journey on the briny deep lives on within the heart of every sailor, attesting to a life of beauty and adventure.

With a full cup of Joe in hand Louis walked out to the terrace and planted himself in a rattan rocker to take in the early morning. The air was so quiet he swore he could hear the blood running through his ears. 'I think they call it tinnitus nowadays,' he thought to himself.

It was very faint at first, and being upwind coming from the mainland, the crescendo of the plane's engine was ever so slow in building. In another minute it was increasing in volume at a greater pace. Louis tried to follow his ears to the sky, but could not spot the approaching plane. Perhaps it had circled around the backside of the high ridge behind the house to the west. Louis got to his feet and looked upward in a 360 sweep and saw nothing as the sound of the plane had diminished completely. The silence returned in a suspended animation as in the start of a race.

When the turboprop DeHavilland Otter broke over the ridge line at treetop height and down the face of the high hill, it

209

gave Louis quite a start. Everyone would soon be awake from the sudden call of that low flyover. Louis kept his gaze on the seaplane as it circled around the bay for a few minutes, and studied the pilot's actions as he was probably lining up the most desirable glide path that would vector him into close proximity with the working research vessel at anchor.

The old captain was familiar with the Otter as he had flown in one more than a few times over the course of his fishing career. It was a powerful single engine turboprop that could carry 8 or 9 passengers into the most remote bodies of water. A highly rated STOL aircraft under most conditions, the Otter could get airborne in less than 1300ft.

The plane had made a final circle when Louis heard the turbo prop power down on a final approach. The pontoons were now throwing white water and the plane was slowing until the pilot powered up to taxi the aircraft to the flat stern of the mothership into a recess that was designed specifically to receive the visitor.

Louis went inside and retrieved the field glasses that were sitting on top of the desk. He pulled out the binoculars from the leather case, and walked back outside and began sighting in all the activity going on aboard the 110 foot work vessel. A young man with a white shirt and epaulets carrying a briefcase was the first to emerge from the plane. He walked up a few steps to the deck of the ship as another man exited the pilot house and offered an extended hand to greet him. Following a brief conversation with each man pointing and gesturing at different spots around Port Royal Bay, the pair went back inside the pilot house.

Louis returned his scan back to the plane and made some mental notes. DeHavilland Otter, flag blue with a white underbelly, Identifying number N76661. He also noticed a bearded, long haired deckie in a wide brimmed hat involved in performing some diving related tasks in the vicinity of the seaplane.

Occasionally, the mate would disappear for a moment and then come back into view lugging scuba tanks and other diving equipment. Louis' eyes remained fixed on the deckhand for as long as he was actively about his work in the vicinity of the seaplane. Satisfied he had observed the activity aboard ship long enough, he walked back inside and set the field glasses atop Mrs. Jennings desk.

"Morning, Honey…that was an interesting wake up call."

~   "Yes it was, Cami, the supply plane Joe was talking about the other day. I was watching the whole thing thru the binoculars didn't seem like anything out of the ordinary. It looked to me like the pilot was just dropping off some paperwork or something to the captain. Hey, so how'd you sleep?"

"Beautifully despite the absence of a good night kiss," Cami replied with a knowing smile.

Louis walked over to her and took her by the hand, "I haven't slept that soundly for as long as I can remember…got more energy than a nineteen year old. Would you like to get a little coffee in you first?" Louis continued to lead her by the hand into the bedroom.

"What and spoil the timing of it all…come on youngster let's see what you got."

Neither had any notion of what time it was when they rose out of bed for the second time that morning, but it was generally agreed that they were starving for a fresh seafood brunch. Louis got another pot of coffee going, and he and Cami settled into a couple of chairs around the circular table on the terrace. She had turned her attention to the research vessel and the occasional activity that came and went in a rather unhurried rhythm. Nobody aboard that rig appeared to be interested in attempting to do much of anything for the moment; standard island time.

"Louie, what did you find in the fridge that Joe might have stashed for us to eat?"

"Kind of rummaging through it now, sweets…aaah….my man Joe left us a nice container full of shrimp salad. Got a few fresh baked rolls over here, add a couple of brewskis and we're in. Wild caught Roatan camaron and the best clear longnecks in the Caribbean for brunch. Life is good…very good indeed."

The pair set a nice table to enjoy the meal and the morning, and even complemented the menu by adding some fresh mango. As they ate quietly their peaceful mood was again stirred by the plane's engine ramping back up. "Well, I guess they've taken care of their business and are booking on out of here," Cami stated with her thumb pointing behind her back.

"Looks that way," replied Louie as he stood and went inside to retrieve the binoculars. He quickly returned and immediately sighted in the Otter, "Let's see what they're up to next over there." Louis gazed intently as the seaplane was aided off the loading dock by a couple of deckhands wielding long staffs who together pushed the craft away from the stern, allowing it to gain headway away from the ship. It continued to taxi away from the mother ship but did not alter speed at all, eventually taxing all the way to the western shore of Port Royal Bay to the second dock over from the Jennings' house; the northernmost drive from the shared cul-de-sac.

Once alongside, a heavy man Louis had not seen all morning emerged from the plane and temporarily cleated the plane's pontoons to the dock as the pilot shut down the engine. All was quiet once again, and Louis continued to monitor the situation as the pilot and heavier man walked the plane closer to shore behind a boat house, and out of his field of vision.

"Now what are they doing I wonder…think I'll give Gillen a call." He put down the field glasses and went to Mrs. Jennings desk and the cell phone.

"Yeah, Louie what's going on?"

"How's it going, Joe, been watching this seaplane all morning, and didn't really think too much of it, that is until it taxied all the way into our shore. A big guy and the pilot proceeded to tie the plane up to the second dock over, you know the one that has the boathouse."

"I got you, cap…DeHavilland Otter, flag blue, white underbelly?"

"That would be the one, Joe."

"Yeah…that's them, not unusual they do that all the time. They come over here to Oak Ridge to grab some fresh lobster and shrimp from the fish house to take back to the mainland. Has the tender followed them over from the ship?"

"Not yet."

"Hmmm…well they'll probably be along sooner than later. Just the same we'll go on yellow alert. I was planning to stop by with the boat in a couple of hours anyway…no worries, Louis."

"All right, Joe, I'll keep an eye out for you."

Louis was finishing up with the kitchen detail when the sound of an outboard coming into the local dock area caught his attention. 'Probably the tender tagging along after the seaplane to assist in loading up the plane for the return trip', Louis figured.

"Cami, take a look over to the dock second over and see if that's Joe or the tender off the research ship, will you, honey."

"Yes, Captain, dear, just going outside with the peepers."

"And...well… what's going on? Hello, Cami."

"Louis, I think you need to come out here for a second."

"Hold on." Louis put the last glass away dried his hands and walked thru the open great room and on out to the terrace. What he encountered was a scene that he had prepared for over and over in his mind for the last year. Now that it was playing out for real before him, he was surprised by the surge in his energy and the sharpening of his senses. He was not surprised at the familiar vapor of cold fear this man's presence always implanted into his gut. The two men with guns trained on Cami offered a beckoning nod of the head to the old captain as if to say, 'Well, skipper what might you have to say for yourself?'

The older of the two men finally cracked that counterfeit smile, "Hello, Captain Gladding, so nice to see you!"

"Sorry I can't return the greeting and say the same to you, Mr. Wendt, as just being in your presence tends to make me rather nauseous."

"Oh…come now good captain, it was always you who insisted I take a more active role in learning how to succeed when out on the water. Remember, Captain Gladding, 'if you want any killing done on this boat, you can do it yourself by starting with that wounded one over there.' You see I took your advice to heart, and so my presence here to complete the task definitely speaks volumes on your ability to teach. I'm really benefiting a great deal from this more active and direct involvement in closing out this project. Sometimes it becomes quite necessary to take back control when that underling you invest in and rely on, is not successful in achieving all the goals of the plan. This new adventure is actually quite invigorating to say the least, Gladding, thank you so much for bringing all this need for correction to my attention."

"Mr. Wendt, ever since we first met at Chub Cay, there has been nothing I could teach you that would do you any good at all. It was made quite clear to me over time that you were a man very much dead in your tracks, and already entangled in spiritual bankruptcy."

"Oh, Captain, don't be so melancholy in your analysis! I am delighted to be here with the two of you together; a nice little bundle that can be gift wrapped and appropriately dispensed with for a fitting grand finale. Why it's absolutely making me giddy. And your trusted mate Crafty, I had no idea he would prove to be so cooperative in making my mission that much easier. He literally spared me a great deal of aggravation and extra planning in his succumbing to his addictions and personal weaknesses."

"What do you truly expect to gain in all this, Wendt?"

"You poor fool, Captain, I have already made tremendous gains beyond your wildest imagination! Now, however, I can enjoy my worldview without your damned nagging presence, finally free of all dangling threads."

"As I have already said, Wendt, you have been completely defeated and are now standing before your grave."

"Yet, I am the one, along with Daniel here, holding you and the lovely Ms. Cami at gunpoint. Humor me…isn't it you who should be considering your own impending mortality? Daniel, escort the lady down to the plane, and if she is uncooperative in any way, knock her out with a shot and load her inside. Danny… no extra-curricular activities please, you and George begin to make things ready with the plane. The captain and I will be along shortly after we have gathered up all their passports, papers and belongings. Go!"

The tender from the research vessel could now be heard making its way over to the same dock where the seaplane had tied up to a few minutes before. The long haired deckie counter-steered the outboard in reverse before shutting it off, allowing the skiff to quietly bob its way in and finally rest against the pier. He made fast with a couple of lines grabbed his sea bag and walked down to the open door of the plane.

"Hello…anybody on board…the captain wanted me to give you guys this bottle of rum from the private stock he had on board. It's the finest kind, great stuff!"

The heavy set occupant stuck his head out the door but only got part of his sentence out, "Thanks, mate, we'd love…," before the deckie pulled out a billy club from the back pocket of his cargo shorts and struck the unsuspecting passenger twice on the side of the head. After the heavy man fell across the open door frame, the deckhand shoved him back inside. He then pulled out a pair of handcuffs from his duffel and affixed the unconscious man to the seat belt mount in the plane's interior. Check.

The deckie grabbed the sea bag and made his way up the hill to the cul-de-sac, and started walking down the driveway leading to the Jennings' house. About thirty yards in he set his sea bag down, and positioned himself behind a preselected clump of palms and other jungle cover, and waited. His heart was beating fast and strong, but it wasn't racing. His combat readiness had kicked in and all his senses were hyperactive and in alert mode. It wasn't long before his ears picked up the activity of someone walking up the Jennings' access road; no talking but the sounds of shoes and sandals displacing the loose gravel could be heard easily.

With the pair probably just a few feet away now, the assailant readied himself for the ambush that required two precise strikes. When the woman cleared his position and came into view, she was walking ahead of her captor by only a few feet. In a blur the mate came down on the gunman's right hand with the backside of a machete, instantly knocking the gun a few feet away into the thick jungle off the side of the road. In an instant, the mate's thumb, index and middle finder locked into a vice grip around the man's larynx as he threw him to the ground. Silently, the young man called Daniel struggled and kicked, making gurgling sounds as his every attempt to breathe was becoming increasingly more difficult. In less than a half minute, the young man's eyes rolled upward and out he went.

The deckie pulled out a second pair of cuffs and fastened the unconscious young man to the biggest palm he could find. He looked over to the wide eyed blonde and silently directed her to be quiet and remain here with the prisoner and then handed her the machete. The mate went into his sea bag and produced the final tool he would need for the end game and began walking the rest of the way down the road towards the house.

The deckie first approached the scene from the terrace steps seeing no one in view inside the house. He ducked behind the double wide chaise when he first became aware of a somewhat muted conversation coming from the front bedroom just off the lodge's great room. The mate quickly covered the short distance to just behind the sliding door frame, and waited for the two men to come into clear view within the main room of the lodge. In stealth mode when the time was right, he would approach the man with the gun from behind.

"All right then that should be everything we need for your little trip, Captain Gladding. Grab your two sea bags and lead the way up the hill please; and do it quickly and quietly before Daniel puts the hurt on your girl."

Barefooted, the deckie silently closed in and crept towards Wendt's backside, then leveled the stainless Ithaca 12 gauge pump directly against his 4th and 5th cervical vertebrae, "How does it feel to be a target Mr. Personality? Drop the piece now, asshole, or just drop dead, makes no difference to me."

Wendt slowly flung the automatic a few feet away, and

slowly turned to meet his captor. "You! You can't… possibly….," was all that the normally expressive Wendt could get out.

In the next moment there appeared khaki everywhere in the form of five policemen who had stormed the house along with the head Constable. Wendt had become nearly catatonic in a daze as he slowly went over and kneeled to pick up his revolver. The mate held the shotgun to the man's head while the others all drew their weapons. However, no one charged or prevented the doomed man from inserting the barrel in his mouth as his final expression captured the unbelief in his eyes. It was over…finally over.

Louis slowly walked over to the bloody mess that was once Adam Wendt, and picked up the gun and handed it to the Police Chief in the white shirt with epaulets. The old captain gave the corpse one final long stare and began to slowly shake his head not in disbelief, but in a somber mood of resignation. Louis then went into the bedroom and grabbed a sheet off the bed to lay over what was left of Adam Wendt.

The deckie lowered his shotgun and discharged the shells before offering it to one of the Chief's men at his side. The mate then removed that wide brimmed hat and ran his hands through his thick mane four or five times before walking over to Louis, "Cami is just fine and she's right up the road safe and sound, cappy."

"Louis grabbed the mate and drew him into a big bear hug, "Crafty, ol'boy, you're a sight to behold, but you really could use a bath and haircut in the worst way!" In another moment, there flowed the laughter and tears of joy upon their spiritual release.

"Chief Belcirst isn't it," Louis introduced himself to the Police Captain.

"Why yessah, you know me from somewhere?"

"Yes," Louis dropped a hand to measure a couple of feet off the floor, "I was Alfie Silva's son when we came to fish here a long time ago, you were only so high."

"I remembah now, my grandfatha' worked at dis place when t'was a fishing lodge many years ago. Very small world indeed, sah," the Chief was really pumping Louis' hand now.

"Samuel, meet my very good friend, Crafty. He is a man of many varied and admirable talents."

"Mr. Crafty it is a pleasure to meet you…de're be no more guns?"

"No, Chief Belcirst, that's it for the guns."

"So…what tipped you off, Crafty?"

"Louis…they were just plain sloppy. I recognized the kid right away, and simply stole a peek into the airplane when they tied up to the ship ramp. I saw the Wendt on his cellphone with a big smirk on his face. He never even looked up."

"Thank you, Lord for watching over us," the old captain stated aloud and he surely did look up.

In about five minute's time, Joe Gillen walked in with Cami in tow and a few more police. Danny boy was still cuffed and appeared considerably weakened by the effects of Crafty's vice grip on his throat.

"Sorry to be a little on the late side, Louie, but we got the job done. Crafty had alerted me from the ship, and I came as soon as I could get here with the boys. We had worked the plan from the moment your mate arrived on the island. Once he alerted us, it was understood that he would go on ahead on point. We just didn't know exactly how all the timing would play out, and how many thugs we'd be dealing with. But no worries then, the vermin have been neutralized. Hallelujah."

Epilogue

Noling's mind was still working overtime, and had been ever since the news had hit the states regarding the death of Adam Wendt. The news media was frothing at the mouth with new headlines and leaders daily, detailing the sordid history behind the planning and staging of the piracy, the murders and of course, the motives of the perpetrators. That it was a larger than life story of the rich betraying the super-rich only stoked the readers' appetite for more details; the headlines and national coverage increased with each passing day. 'Corporate Capital and Greed, 'When Is Enough, Enough?'

Danny Boy and George, the fat Texan, had been extradited to Noling's jurisdiction in West Palm Beach, and the Federal Marshalls tied a big red ribbon around that Spencer sportfish and sealed it to the dock for the time being. The Otter had also been seized as well even though it hadn't actually been stolen. Wendt's partners in crime in Tegucigalpa had connections to the regular carrier that serviced the research vessel and merely substituted another plane, painted and numbered to duplicate the original.

The detective laughed out loud as he continued to mull over his notes and the circumstances of this investigation, and the various trails they left for him and others to follow; it's why he loved his work so much. 'Nothing is ever as it first appears' was probably the only guidance he had truly lived by in all his years as a cop. More fun than a treasure hunt, he loved and lived for those rare moments when things first came to light. As far as Noling was concerned every crime was already a completed jigsaw puzzle someone had thrown up against the wall. Lead or be led it mattered little, just find all the damn pieces. "No wonder I like fishing so much you never know what's going to happen in the next second," Noling reflected out loud as he rose from his desk

He walked down the hall and stopped to glance into the interrogation room where all his invited 'guests' were seated around the drab gray table talking among themselves. 'Quite a garden party' he thought to himself, though by now he had acquired a certain sense of kinship with the folks. It felt good to unburden these victims of despair from their unseen tormenter. The detective took a moment to be thankful for the way things worked out in the end before reaching for the door.

"Hello everyone, I'd like to personally thank you all for keeping me so busy and entertained these past couple of weeks. Is there a chance any of you have ever dabbled in some manner of detective work of your own?"

"Catching fish…catching people…it ain't really that much different is it?" Frankie barely got the jab out before breaking down in laughter. "Anyway, detective, we are all in your debt for everything you've done in handling the case."

"Right, Captain…I haven't done much of anything, really."

"Well, you haven't thrown any of us in the slammer yet," Cami observed.

"That is true, Ms. Letourneau…giving false testimony to a law enforcement officer is a criminal offense. First off, Mr. Kraft… I need to know how were you able to do such a convincing job of faking your own death."

"Frankie's wife works in the ER over at St Mary's, Detective. When I took Emory over there to get his shoulder worked on, I just suddenly got this inspiration. If I could stage my own death I could really turn the table on Wendt by being that much more effective in stalking him. I was done playing cat and mouse, and being a target was really getting old. So, a few of us working together went into a plan to drop a bait back by laying a little trail for him. Now we could direct his efforts more in concert, and plan for the day when, hopefully, it would all come together. Kind of like sitting in a deer stand, at least we knew where he would be coming from."

"You already suspected Wendt then," Noling pressed on.

"From the very beginning, but we didn't want to tip our hand," Louis added.

"More false testimony from you too, eh Captain Gladding? I must say, however, that early on Wendt was the prime suspect in my mind as well," Noling confessed.

"Given the lack of hard evidence, detective, how did you come to that conclusion tying him to the piracy?"

"Captain Gladding….it was not anything specific he said in his testimony, but rather what he didn't say. When I asked you and Ms. Letourneau to suggest a motive for the crime, you touched on all the bases; kidnapping, ransom, espionage, corporate Intel and so on. When I posed the same question to Mr. Wendt he limited his answer to kidnapping and ransom, before shedding a few crocodile tears. He was unconsciously blocked from citing any other reasons as a way of taking the attention away from the true motive for the crime, corporate espionage. Getting back to you Mr. Kraft, how were you able to fabricate such a convincing crime scene? I mean…what about the blood, the sandals, disposing of the 'now dead' body?"

"Like I said, Frankie's wife is a nurse over there at St. Mary's. I just went over there and had her draw some blood from me over the course of a few nights; just enough to create a scene of tragedy. We planned to do it on the new moon with the dark night and stronger tides. A couple of the bait fishermen just cruised by the boat, stuck me under the tarp and ran me up Lake Worth to Frankie's boat, where I was then shipped off to the Keys. I stayed at the Silva house until I hitched a ride to Cozumel with one of the guys heading down. From there I contacted Joe in Roatan and came down on a supply ship the rest of the way. All along the way we set little crumbs out hoping that we left a believable trail. The key was not letting anyone know too much. The kid, Alfie Silva, yourself, even Flores and the Gloves; you all had a hand in steering Wendt and his people into our trap."

"Who was in on your scheme, you know, your end of things?"

"The only people who truly knew I had faked my death were Louis, Emory, Frankie, Alfie, the Gloves and the two bait fishermen who shall remain anonymous. We decided not to tell the Greek, Cami or anyone else for that matter as it might have diluted the illusion.

"What about Flores? Then there were those two brothers, and all those headlines of legal wrangling and no-growth development. The damn media with those daily editorials, you'd have thought they might have accidentally uncovered something or in the very least got in the way of your elaborate scheme."

"From the beginning, the media were blinded from the criminal side of the piracy by focusing all their coverage on the political angle. They were also indifferent to the tripwires the McDade brothers set for Wendt and his partners. The only angle they pursued was the environmental impact to public lands and waters, all under the control of land owners, state and federal politicians. Well they got about as much out of that story as they were interested in at the time, don't you think? I'm sure they had their own reasons for not initially digging deeper into the life and times of Adam Wendt. You know detective…sometimes you'll get a nice fish up to your bait spread and the damn creature just won't eat. He might kick hard, he might light up his pectoral fins and tail, he might check out every bait in the entire spread, but he just won't make his move and eat. Sometimes you just have to sting him a little, you know, piss him off. One great way to piss off a window shopper is to snatch that bait right away from him, isn't that right Louie."

Louis nodded in agreement, "That's what we attempted to do with the bait and switch on Mr. Wendt, Detective. We gave him a little scent of our whereabouts and then hit the trail."

"All right, boys, I'm getting a tad dizzy from all this, but you have made some good points there. I do believe after all this criminology and character analysis, that I could be more than a little ready for some time on the water."

"Well sir, we were all throwing it around before you walked in," the Greek answered, "and the decision was unanimous. My crew and the ladies would like to take you fishing on my boat as a guest charter. So what say you, Detective Noling?"

"What a truly fine idea people, I got no problem with that whatsoever. There is one guy down at Customs and Border Protection I'd like to bring along if that's all right."

The Greek cracked a big smile, "Your call, Sir, it's your charter."

* * * * * *

It was a wet and windy gray day with squall lines moving onshore every thirty minutes. The third tropical system of the month was slowly and stubbornly hanging on as the rain bands continued to drench south Florida with another ten inches of rain from the backside of its circulation. Not exactly a chamber of commerce weather pattern, the month long deluge had filled the big lake to a dangerously high level well over fifteen feet. The need to protect the integrity of the Hoover Dike mandated constant releases from the high water level, and the flood gates remained wide open day and night at all the locks east and west. Brown silted water heavily laden with runoff and nutrients was gushing in currents exceeding those of the Gulf Stream towards the bio-sensitive estuaries on Florida's west and east coast.

Normally quite saline and clear, the estuarine environment is critical to the reproduction and survival rates of countless marine fish, shellfish and other species that rely on the inshore food chain for their very existence. This assault on these precious bodies of water would leave them void of the majority of sea life normally living within them. Sea grasses would be wiped out for months, possibly years, and the oysters that clean and strain as part of their place in the system would all perish in vast numbers.

All ecological balance is upended. Salt estuaries and ocean inlets go from clean saline ocean water to brown fresh silted muck. Florida Bay which by design is a delicately balanced clean brackish body of water becomes overly saline when deprived of the southerly flow of fresh water from Okeechobee down through the Everglades. The escalating salinity level inhibits sea grass growth and eventually breaks down existing grasses into a compromised state. The aquifer is not charged through percolation the glades would normally provide; salt water begins to encroach where fresh water once was the norm. In terms of making an engineering assessment, it quite possibly could be the most abhorrent and disastrous management of a perfect and natural ecosystem of beauty, at the hands of man.

Henry Flores and Big Jim McCravy ate quietly as they picked through their lobster and cracked conch. Neither man had much to say for even the weather which had been unsettled for so long, had become a boring topic of conversation. It was too inclement to walk out to the beach, and the normally turquoise surf had been replaced by an expanse of the brown sludge resulting from the constant fresh water releases from the big lake.

When the plates had all been cleared, Flores turned his gaze to the gray and brown ocean and just stared for a while. Big Jim had never seen the man so quiet and reserved. The minutes passed slowly in silence before Flores finally turned back to his guest measuring his words for a moment.

"This is exactly how I thought the Californian would end up. He was reckless and to a large degree, unaware of the forces that drive this world, don't you think, Jim?"

"He was certainly all of that, Henry, it didn't seem like 'respect' was a word in his vocabulary. But he's gone now, sir, and with that reckoning we can now move on once again.

"I suppose so, Jim, since as you say he's not going to be a problem for us anymore," replied the sugar baron in an unusually somber tone while still gazing out to sea. Flores continued to stare out at the dark gray horizon and appeared completely incapable of taking the conversation any further. He looked back at Big Jim and then turned away once more, back to the sound of the surf. "Then why is my heart so sore on this gray day I ask myself. I do not like to see the ocean so injured like this; it has played such an important role in my life and given me so many wonderful memories. This is not how I want to remember her or myself for that matter. I have been very fortunate in moving to this country, and I see clearly that it wasn't I who constructed all this flawed engineering a long time ago. But you know, Jim…to him who much is given, much is expected, yes."

"These are always hard times for us at water management when the rain cycle becomes extreme and out of balance. Things will improve, Henry, they always do. As you have always noted, we kind of inherited this system so we were forced to work within its constraints. Wouldn't that be a fair statement sir?"

The Cuban suddenly rose to his feet and straightened out his white shirt and addressed his guest with full eye contact. "What you say is very true, Big Jim, but there have been subtle changes over the years regarding the nature of our relationship, and the generosity we share with the governments in Tallahassee and Washington. I am thinking that things have quietly tipped far more in favor of the politicians who desire to extract more and more from this equation. I do not like this trend that I am beginning to sense."

"They support us in every conceivable way, Henry."

"They are dragging their feet on the southern flow way; we have canals east and west… we can certainly have a canal going through my land where there once was one. I can work the numbers, take and back pump water to and from that southern river just as in the lake, and it won't overly cripple production in the long run. You see, Jim, I can cut a river south and I can easily manage all my water needs from such a river. The water will always be there moving through. Flores waved his arm to the sea in disgust and started away from the table, "At least I won't have to look out at all that!"

The Cuban silently stared out to sea for another few minutes before slowly making his way to the open sliding door. He reappeared after a brief moment from the slider to address Big Jim once more, "Jim, I see too many things coming to a collision, and even this once useful relationship will eventually fail in the end. I can lose only a slice of my land, but gain a great amount of political capital. To that end, I would rather be the first to do so ahead of the politicians. Put a call into Tallahassee and ask somebody up there why in hell they are sitting on their hands, and redirecting the taxpayers' money which was earmarked in a statewide vote. Better yet...find out where it went or where they stashed it. Can you do that for me, Jim?"

"It's worth a shot, Henry...and the timing just might work out very well for you and your brother. Why the hell not!"

Flores made one long last scan of the ocean. "I am... becoming...tired of all this!" was all the Cuban said as he activated the sliding door behind him.

The hopes and prayers of the many, have now been duly noted.